"I sensed some…

He glanced at the cei[ling] vocabulary then clicked his fingers as he found the right word. "Hostility from you."

"Hostility?"

He nodded, inflaming her further. "I thought we could behave like adults, but one minute you're dismissing my invitation, the next changing your mind."

"I was not being hostile. I think the word you actually mean is 'circumspection.' I was being respectful of our working relationship." But of course, she had dismissed him, out of fear and nerves and sheer panic.

Sadie tried to stay aloof with him, but the absurdity of their bickering finally registered and she laughed it off with a shake of her head.

When she looked up, he was smiling.

"So, will you meet me for a drink or not?" she asked, dragging in a shuddering breath, because this Roman was the man she'd flirted with in Vienna. A straight-up, say-it-like-it-is, intelligent and funny guy who would surely react positively to the news that he had a daughter.

Wouldn't he…?

Dear Reader,

I hope you enjoy this Valentine's Day medical story. I loved flinging betrayed Sadie and tortured Roman into an Anti-Valentine's Party at the start of the book. They were both so smug, both certain that they wanted nothing to do with love. Of course, it's not over until the final chapter, and everyone deserves a second chance. Fortunately for Roman and Sadie, Valentine's Day happens every year...

Enjoy!

Love,

JC xx

HER SECRET
VALENTINE'S BABY

———

JC HARROWAY

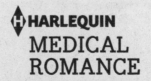

HARLEQUIN
MEDICAL
ROMANCE

HARLEQUIN®
MEDICAL ROMANCE™

Recycling programs
for this product may
not exist in your area.

ISBN-13: 978-1-335-59523-2

Her Secret Valentine's Baby

Copyright © 2024 by JC Harroway

For questions and comments about the quality of this book, please contact us at CustomerService@Harlequin.com.

Harlequin Enterprises ULC
22 Adelaide St. West, 41st Floor
Toronto, Ontario M5H 4E3, Canada
www.Harlequin.com

Printed in U.S.A.

Lifelong romance addict **JC Harroway** took a break from her career as a junior doctor to raise a family and found her calling as a Harlequin author instead. She now lives in New Zealand and finds that writing feeds her very real obsession with happy endings and the endorphin rush they create. You can follow her at jcharroway.com and on Facebook, Twitter and Instagram.

Books by JC Harroway

Harlequin Medical Romance

A Sydney Central Reunion
Phoebe's Baby Bombshell

Gulf Harbour ER
Tempted by the Rebel Surgeon
Breaking the Single Mom's Rules

Forbidden Fling with Dr. Right
How to Resist the Single Dad

Visit the Author Profile page
at Harlequin.com for more titles.

To my smart, beautiful and kind daughter.
Thanks for the office and the hugs xx

CHAPTER ONE

Valentine's Day

Dr Sadie Barnes was in no mood for the party filling Vienna's Danube Hotel bar. She almost turned tail. Just her luck to encounter a group of rowdy singletons on her first Valentine's Day alone for six years.

She needed wine, stat.

Ducking her head, she bypassed the loved-up gathering and headed for the bar, where she intended to order the largest glass of white possible in her stilted German. Somewhere back in London, her ex was celebrating lovers' day with his shiny new, pregnant fiancée, the woman he'd cheated on Sadie with.

On any other day, she'd have headed straight upstairs to her room, especially after a long day of lectures and networking at the Progress in Paediatrics medical conference at the hospital across the road. Instead, she placed her order with the bartender and took a seat far away from the party, wearily sagging into the barstool.

Why was it, when you'd been horribly betrayed and humiliated, your heart thrashed to pieces, so easy to believe that every other person on the planet was blissfully in love?

Realising that she had veered into a cynical and self-indulgent wallow, Sadie thanked the bartender for her glass of wine. *'Vielen dank.'*

He smiled what might have been a flirtatious smile.

Sadie looked away, took a huge gulp of Sauvignon Blanc, no longer able to trust her instincts where men were concerned after Mark's broken promises. Better to focus her energy on work, on today's highly informative symposium, on returning to London tomorrow refreshed and professionally reinvigorated, this nauseating, love-drenched day over for another year.

If only the Valentine's revellers would let her forget.

The bar resounded with a series of loud bangs as multiple confetti cannons were discharged into the air. Sadie jumped, her hand flying to her chest as hundreds of pink and red paper hearts fluttered down on the cheering crowd.

She hadn't realised that she'd actually released the groan of irritation aloud until the man next to her at the bar spoke.

'That's two sighs in the space of a minute,' he said, causing Sadie to notice him for the first time where he'd been previously obscured by a pillar, as if he too wanted to distance himself from the party.

'But don't worry,' he continued in excellent but accented English. 'Hopefully, that's as raucous as they'll get.'

'I hope so.' Sadie nodded, carefully observing her fellow party pooper from behind her wine glass.

Broad-chested, dark-haired and with kind blue eyes, he was undeniably the kind of man any woman with a pulse would notice. But she'd been so wrapped up in her private pity-fest, she'd been blind to the hottie skulking with her in the corner.

'It wouldn't normally bother me,' Sadie said with a third sigh, 'but I came in to be alone, for a quiet drink.'

A drink to help her forget that there wouldn't be a red envelope on her doormat when she returned to her flat. Mark had always ostentatiously marked the romance of Valentine's Day year after year—a dozen red roses, surprise trips to Paris, candlelit dinners… But his grand declarations and overt shows of affection had been a baseless charade, as if Sadie had been a place keeper, a stand-in until someone better had come along.

'Me too.' The stranger's sexy mouth kicked up with a hint of a conspiratorial smile that turned him from good-looking to drop-dead gorgeous.

He raised his glass in solidarity and settled back behind the pillar, making it obvious that he had no intention of hitting on Sadie.

Deflated, she took a second look.

Maybe because he was so clearly uninterested in flirting, maybe because her loneliness was heightened by the rowdy celebration, maybe because she was so utterly done with relationships after Mark's hurtful betrayal, Sadie found herself eager to prolong the harmless conversation.

'Instead,' she said, drawing his attention once more, 'we find ourselves in the middle of a Valentine's party. There should be a law against that kind of thing.'

Matching her smile for smile, the handsome stranger this time eyed her with definite interest.

'Anti-Valentine's party,' he corrected, pointing to a heart-festooned poster behind the bar, which clearly advertised the event.

She dragged her stare from his intense eye contact to ponder the poster, which was written in German way beyond her translational skills.

'What's an Anti-Valentine's party?' she asked, intrigued. 'Ordering a drink is about the limit of my capabilities. As you can probably tell, I'm not a local.'

'Me neither,' he said, sliding his stool to her side of the pillar so they could talk without a barrier. 'I'm Czech, but I also speak German, so allow me to translate.'

Sadie nodded, mesmerised by his deep-voiced, accented English. Now she was faced with the close-up of his strong jaw darkened with stubble, the ghost of a smile on his distracting lips and his blue eyes dancing with humour, the tension in her body that she hadn't been aware of melted away.

'It says "Anti-Valentine's Party Rules".' He leaned sideways to read the poster, wafting Sadie with his delicious spicy aftershave.

The sexy Czech was around ten years older than her thirty-two, his smile deepening the crinkles at the corners of his eyes, which were framed by a dignified scatter of grey hair at his temples.

Fascinated that for the first time since her break-up seven months ago, Sadie could imagine herself flirting with this man, she took another gulp of wine to hide her body's unexpected swoon and nodded for him to continue the translation.

'"Rule number one,"' Blue Eyes said. '"You must be single."'

Shrugging one broad shoulder in a way that said it was pretty self-explanatory, he paused, waiting expectantly for Sadie's answer.

Was he flirting with her?

'Tick,' she said, emphasising her unavailability by drawing the symbol in the air with a nervous chuckle.

The man helping her to forget that her ex was as shallow as a puddle copied her gesture with a playful smile that left Sadie scoping out evidence of a wedding ring on his hand, only to be pleasantly exhilarated by its absence.

Was she flirting with *him*?

Even more shocking was how the idea fizzed pleasantly through her veins.

Why shouldn't she flirt with a smart, attractive single man? Just because her ex had cast her aside despite his grand protestations and empty promises, didn't mean that Sadie couldn't once more enjoy feeling desired.

'"Rule number two,"' her companion continued, leaning closer as he read so Sadie was aware of his body heat, a thrill of excitement waking up her nervous system. '"You aren't looking for a relationship."'

'So far so good,' Sadie said as she and her mystery man ticked the air in unison, their stares colliding and holding so tingles ping-ponged around inside her belly.

He *was* flirting with her.

Thrills of delight snaked down her spine. Just because Mark had thrown her away didn't make her worthless. Yes, she had her…issues, ones that Mark had denied were a problem when they'd first met, but she could still attract a man if she so chose. The right man, of course, one who shared her new philosophy on avoiding commitment.

'What about rule number three?' she asked, her smile gaining confidence.

This was the longest rule of the three and Sadie waited with bated breath, now fully invested in the idea of this stupid party given that this sexy and unexpected man obviously shared her relationship aversion.

But was it any wonder that she would lap up the attention of a kind and handsome stranger after being so callously discarded by a man who'd claimed to love her? Perhaps it was time she had a fling to put her ex's rejection and her decimated instincts well and truly in the past.

'"Rule number three,"' he continued. '"No…" How do you say…?' He waved his hand, spoke a few words in what Sadie assumed was Czech, as if he was struggling with the exact translation.

Sadie foolishly watched his lips as they mouthed the German words, torturing herself by calculating the two hundred and eighteen days it had been since she'd been kissed.

Long, lonely days filled with self-doubt that, because of her fertility issues, no one would ever want her again.

Having figured it out, he said, '"No hookups…unless you are prepared to risk being lured to the dark side of red roses, broken hearts and shattered expectations when the phone stays silent…" Or something along those lines.'

'Oh…' A stab of disappointment jabbed at her ribs. Even though she agreed with the sentiment, Sadie couldn't bring herself to make a tick this time, keeping her fingers wrapped around the stem of her wine glass.

'Well, thanks for the translation,' she said, studying the liquid left in the glass, hoping to hide her crestfallen expression that they wouldn't be taking their fun flirtation to the next level.

'It turns out that this *is* my kind of party after all, but I think I'll give it a miss anyway…' she prattled on, not daring to look his way. That last rule had dumped a bucket of iced water on her fantasy of hooking up with this like-minded stranger.

Except now that the idea was out there, it was stuck in her mind like a deep splinter.

'I just came in for a drink after a long day.' She waved her hand at her near empty glass of wine. 'I'm leaving Vienna in the morning…so a party probably isn't a good idea.'

She always over-talked when she was nervous, and he was the first man in a long time to make her nervous.

'But what about you?' She finally braved eye contact. 'Tempted to join the other cynics and commitment-phobes?'

To stop her mouth making more unnecessary words, she gulped her drink, trying to forget how, for a few minutes, while they'd flirted and learned how much they had in common when it came to love and relationships and the dreaded Valentine's Day, this compelling man had made her feel attractive again, whole, hopeful that she'd be okay, even if it was alone.

His stare lingered, sending shivers of anticipation down her limbs.

His answer, when it came, was delivered with quiet intensity that left Sadie in no doubt of his sincerity.

'I can't be lured to the dark side,' he stated flatly, cryptically. 'All that love and relationship stuff is for people hoping to find *the one* and start a family. That's not me.'

He shrugged, the slight hunch to his broad shoulders, the flicker of sadness in his blue eyes telling her that they might have much more in common than either of them had realised when they struck up this conversation.

Sadie froze as his frown-pinched gaze traced her face, pausing at her mouth in a disconcerting way. Was he, like Sadie, gutted about rule number three? Had he, too, been considering a one-night stand with a stranger to banish the loneliness?

'Me neither,' she whispered, fighting the absurd urge to reach out and touch his arm, to comfort and be comforted, certain that they each had painful reasons for being alone tonight.

A different kind of tension sparked between them, an awareness, recognition, a breathless moment of possibility.

Galvanised by memories of her ex's excuses and lies, by the hurtful truth of his betrayal, which had damaged the self-acceptance she'd worked hard for following her diagnosis of infertility in her twenties, Sadie bravely raised her glass.

'Well, cheers to us and down with Valentine's Day,' she said.

Just because she couldn't be a mother, didn't diminish her as a woman. This sexy stranger had helped her to cement that conclusion tonight. She had a good life, a career she loved, her family and friends.

With an unflinching gaze, he touched his glass to hers. 'To us.'

Holding his stare while they each took a sip, Sadie searched for relief that their flirtation would go no further, only to be pleasantly frustrated.

She didn't know his name. She hadn't been

looking to meet him and would most likely never see him again. Only she sensed an affinity with this intriguing man. And something in his eyes told her he felt it too.

'Well, it was lovely to meet a like-minded romance sceptic,' she finally said, noticing that the party had all but disbanded, the staff clearing away glasses and sweeping up paper hearts from the floor.

Almost reluctantly, she slid from her stool and held out her hand for him to shake, forcing herself to walk away. As much as she found this stranger wildly attractive, as much as she'd resolved to move on, she hadn't slept with anyone but her ex in six and a half years.

But maybe she should.

Mark was in London with his pregnant fiancée, most certainly *not* thinking about Sadie tonight.

Her stranger stood too, taking her hand so her stomach flipped at his warm and confident touch. 'It's been an unexpected pleasure—the best Anti-Valentine's Valentine's Day I've had in years.'

Sadie laughed, beyond flattered.

Although he smiled warmly, he regarded her as he had done all evening—with self-assured interest and a quiet calm she found so appealing after Mark's effusive but empty promises.

'Good luck staying single,' she said, her heart hammering so hard he would surely hear it.

'You too.' He leaned in and kissed her cheek in that European way, the soft brush of his lips agonisingly brief, the scrape of his stubbled jaw thrilling, the warmth of his body enticing her to admit how comfortable she felt with him, how similar they were, how easy it would be to surrender to this unexpected and fierce attraction.

Her hand was still clasped in his, neither of them pulling away as they faced each other. Vulnerable but safe. Strangers but somehow also allies against the folly of love.

Sadie stared into his blue eyes, the word goodbye trapped in her throat. Her resolve wavered back and forth. Was there an old condom in the bottom of her wash bag? Was she wearing the tattiest underwear she owned? Could they keep tonight anonymous and regret-free?

'Although I was thinking…' she said, emboldened by the fact neither of them had moved away, by the fascination and heat in his stare, 'that for a couple of committed singletons like us, we're probably safe to break rule three.'

'Definitely safe,' he said, his irises darkening by a few shades to denim blue. 'If you're sure…?'

His fingers gripped her hand a little tighter, his index finger swiping the pulse point on her inner wrist in hypnotic circles that almost buckled Sadie's knees with desire.

If that simple touch could ignite her libido so dramatically, how would things be between them when the clothes came off?

She couldn't wait to find out.

'Who needs Valentine's, right?' she whispered, still holding his hand as they headed for the hotel lifts.

'Not us,' he said as the lift doors closed.

He pulled her into his arms, cupping her face with one hand. 'You're beautiful.' Tugging her hair loose from its ponytail so he could tangle his hands there, he tilted up her face.

Sadie feared she might pass out. But then his lips crashed to hers in a desperate rush.

She moaned into their kiss, parted her lips, and welcomed the thrust of his tongue, glad that she'd trusted this particular instinct. Had she ever felt this instantly attracted to someone? So powerfully turned on?

She became aware of movement—the lift ascending, or her knees finally buckling, or the earth shifting on its axis like a romantic cliche. But then her fingers were tangled in his hair to direct his kiss deeper. Her back was somehow against the wall of the lift and his thigh was pressed between her parted legs while his hand cupped her breast through her blouse, toying the nipple into a taut peak.

This wasn't about romance. It was need, pure and simple. His and hers in flawless harmony.

The lift doors opened.

Flames chased them down the hall.

Sadie hurriedly fumbled with the electronic key card while he nuzzled kisses along her neck and gripped her hips from behind, his erection pressed to the small of her back.

With her groan of relief, the door gave way and they tumbled inside the room.

There was no time to activate the lights as they discarded their shoes and kissed their way over to the bed. No time for Sadie to worry about the state of her underwear as they frantically stripped off, kissed and touched as much of each other's bodies as they could. And no need to worry about protection as he reached for his wallet before covering her naked body with his on the bed.

'I hate Valentine's Day,' she panted out as he took one nipple into his mouth and sucked, sliding his hand between her legs.

This was so much better than she'd imagined, everything about him, from his ripped naked form and impressive arousal to the way he instinctively seemed to know how to set her body alight with his touch, perfect.

'Worst day ever,' he agreed, pressing a trail

of hot kisses down her ribs and stomach before settling between her legs to pleasure her with his mouth.

Except two condoms, four orgasms and one goodbye kiss later, Sadie knew without a shadow of a doubt that it was one Valentine's Day she would never forget.

CHAPTER TWO

Eleven months later...

SLIGHTLY OUT OF breath from rushing to be on time for her first day back at work, Sadie paused at Sunshine Ward's reception desk, greeting staff she hadn't seen for the four months she'd been away on maternity leave.

'Pictures, please,' Sister Samuels, or Sammy as she preferred to be called, demanded with a smile, holding out her hand until Sadie obliged by unlocking and then handing over her phone.

While Sammy and a small cluster of other nurses oohed and ahhed at baby photos, Sadie tried to stave off the pangs of heartache and guilt for leaving her two-month-old daughter, Milly, the tiny miracle that had turned her world upside down in the best way imaginable.

Sadie itched to grab her phone back. She'd only been back at work for five minutes, and already she wanted to call her twin sister, Grace, who was a qualified nanny, and check up on the baby. But there was no one she trusted more than her twin. They'd shared a uterus, for goodness' sake.

'She's adorable,' Sammy said, handing back Sadie's phone before answering the ward phone, while handing over the keys to the drug cupboard to another of the paediatric nurses, multitasking like a pro.

Praying that Milly would be fine—after all, Grace had more or less moved in with them the minute Milly was born, and Sadie had expressed enough breast milk to feed an army of babies— she turned her mind to work.

It was the usual hectic Monday morning at London Children's Hospital.

While Sadie waited for Sammy to end her phone call so they could begin a ward round together, she settled at a free computer terminal, logged on and opened her work emails.

Unsurprisingly, her inbox was chock-a-block. Filtering out the staff memos and hospital newsletters, she worked her way through what was left, mentally prioritising the list, and postponing anything non-urgent until later in the day.

One email marked 'Urgent' caught her attention. She clicked on it, groaning when the attachment downloaded—a red heart-festooned poster advertising the hospital's Valentine's Day Fund-raising Auction, which was being held in three weeks' time.

Distractedly, Sadie scanned the adjoining message:

...welcome back...you have been allocated a role as one of the auctioneers on the night... here's the list of donations/auctions...

Sadie sighed—clearly, in her absence, she'd been given a job no one else wanted. What with caring for baby Milly and returning to work, the hyped-up hullabaloo of Valentine's Day wasn't even on her radar. She was a single mum and a part-time paediatric registrar at the UK's busiest children's hospital. The last thing she needed was the added work of this romantic nonsense.

Not to mention the reminder of last Valentine's...

A hot flush crept up her neck as flashes of erotic memories popped behind her eyes. That man had seriously rocked her world. And talk about fertile...

'I'm sorry you got lumbered with auctioneer.' Sammy spoke over Sadie's shoulder. 'We drew straws for jobs.' Sammy winced.

Sadie waved off the older woman's explanation, relieved to have something else to think about other than a pair of intense blue eyes, voracious lips, a night of unbridled pleasure that had resulted in her precious baby.

'It's okay. It's for a good cause, right?' Distractedly, Sadie scanned the list of auctions, which among other things boasted a couples skydive and a week's break in Tuscany.

Impatient to begin her review of the current inpatients on the ward, Sadie logged out of her emails. While she wanted the hospital fundraiser to be a success, she wouldn't be wasting too much of her precious time on other people's love lives.

Now, more than ever, she had different priorities: her daughter.

Sammy grabbed one of the ward tablets from the charging station, telling Sadie, to her relief, she was ready to begin the ward round.

Except her reprieve was short-lived; it seemed the Valentine's fundraiser was the hot topic of conversation.

'If we can raise enough money,' Sammy continued as they headed for the far end of the ward, 'the proceeds will fund a new state-of-the-art sensory playroom and a much-needed makeover of the family room.'

'That's great.' Sadie smiled, torn between wanting to help and justifying anything that took her away from her time with Milly. There was no denying that the fundraiser was very much needed. Play was an important part of a child's healthy recovery and the family room served multiple purposes from a place for parents to relax to the venue where some families heard the worst news imaginable.

But her precious daughter was a miracle she'd long ago stopped hoping for after she'd been diagnosed with primary ovarian insufficiency in her twenties, a diagnosis Mark had claimed hadn't mattered. Until it had. Until he'd cheated and conceived with another woman.

But then, just when she'd finally put his betrayal behind her, Sadie had met a mysterious Czech stranger in a Viennese bar.

'Besides,' Sammy said, pausing at the whiteboard, which listed the current inpatients by name and designated consultant, the place where all ward rounds began, 'as an auctioneer, you'll have the inside details on the auctions before everyone else.'

Sammy winked, knowingly.

'Oh, I won't be bidding on any of the prizes.' Sadie flushed. 'I've just had a baby.'

No one except Grace knew anything about Milly's paternity and Sadie intended to keep it that way.

'I have no use for a couple's massage,' Sadie scoffed, nervous under Sammy's keen scrutiny, 'or a romantic dinner for two, unless there's baby food on the menu.'

'I know,' said Sammy, briskly wiping the names of those patients discharged overnight from the whiteboard and updating the number of free beds available for the day's new admissions, 'but you're successful, attractive and single.'

Sammy phrased the word as a question, still fishing for a clue about Milly's father, ever the romantic at heart.

'You should never say never,' Sammy concluded, turning away from the whiteboard.

'Nope.' Sadie shook her head, adamant. Dating was still the last thing on her mind. That amazing night with her mystery man changed nothing. Abiding by the rules of the Anti-Valentine's party, they'd shared a few hours of passion and then parted ways without even sharing their names.

It had been perfect.

Now Sadie had moved on from her ex's betrayal and moved on from that anonymous night, her life taking a wonderful new direction. And if she occasionally, that was daily, wondered about the man who'd donated his blue eyes to her beloved daughter, she quickly set such pointless curiosity aside, too embarrassed to admit to anyone but her sister that she'd had a one-night stand with a man she couldn't even begin to track down to let him know he was a father.

'I have everything I need in my baby girl and my job, thank you very much.' Unlike with a romantic relationship, when it came to motherhood, Sadie didn't have to worry about trust or rejection. Milly's love was unconditional. So there was no father on the scene—Sadie could focus on being everything Milly needed.

'Not even tempted by the main prize,' Sammy pushed, 'the one you'll be auctioning, the one everyone is furiously saving up to win?'

At Sadie's blank expression, the senior nurse elaborated, making dramatic finger quotes. '"A date with an eligible doctor".'

'No, thank you. Definitely not.' Sadie snorted, wheeling the laptop trolley into the first six-bed bay of patients.

She'd take warm baby snuggles and sick stains on her shirt over being let down by a man any day. Not that she in any way blamed her Czech lover for impregnating her, in fact she would always be grateful to the man for the most wondrous of gifts. And at least this way, alone, she didn't have the distraction of a relationship, the worry that she was being lied to, cheated on or unfavourably compared to another woman.

'Who on earth did you find to volunteer for that, anyway?' Sadie asked, smirking. 'The poor guy will be eaten alive. I hope someone has thought about security on the night, because it's going to be carnage.'

Paediatrics attracted a certain kind of doctor, and a hot single man who was good with children was sure to set both ovaries and hearts aflutter.

Sammy flashed her ruthlessly persuasive smile. 'Let's just say that he was coerced rather than volunteered. But Dr Ježek, our new locum surgeon, was happy to have his arm twisted for a good cause.'

Sadie rolled her eyes at the nurse's Machiavellian tactics, already feeling a little sorry for the poor, unsuspecting guy, who was clearly a good sport and might not be aware exactly what he'd signed up for.

'You might change your mind about bidding on that auction when you see him.' Sammy winked and fanned her face, girlishly.

'Not interested.' Sadie drew to a halt at the foot of the first bed, determined to remain the only single woman in a fifty-mile radius of the hospital to stay immune to the kind of man who would volunteer to have women fighting over him, outbidding each other for a date.

'Right, let's start the ward round,' she said, bringing up the notes of the first patient on her list. The sooner she started work, the sooner the day would fly by so she could rush home to Milly.

Sadie and Sammy had reviewed three patients and marked two of them for discharge when the ward alarm sounded. Leaving everything, Sadie rushed to the emergency, adrenaline coursing through her veins, with Sammy hot on her heels.

They entered the bay where the curtains had been drawn around the bed. The nurse caring for the bed's occupant looked up gratefully, her expression alarmed.

'This is Abigail Swift—Abby—six years old,' the nurse said, lowering the head of the bed while she spoke. 'She's one day post-op for laparoscopic repair of intestinal intussusception.'

Sadie took Abby's rapid pulse, noting that she was conscious, but groggy, her colour a worrying shade of grey.

'Blood pressure has been on the low side overnight,' Abby's nurse continued, 'but it just dropped further while we were mobilising Abby. There was a brief loss of consciousness.'

While Sadie spoke to Abby, introducing herself and reassuring the little girl, noting the sweat on her brow, someone turned up a dial on the wall, adjusting the oxygen supply through Abby's mask.

While Sadie placed a hand on Abby's abdomen, Sammy increased the rate of the intravenous infusion. Sadie checked the cardiac monitor, seeing that the girl's heart was in a normal rhythm but she was tachycardic and hypotensive, an indication that she was in shock and was most likely bleeding internally.

'Let's get some more IV fluids.' Sadie reached for an IV cannula and inserted it into Abby's free arm. 'And an urgent cross match for blood transfusion, please.'

She drew a sample of blood for the lab, worried that Abby might have a serious post-operative complication and that she might crash again at any minute. Sammy began infusing the additional intravenous fluids through the new cannula, squeezing the IV bag to speed things along. They needed to get Abby's blood pressure up. Fast.

'Has the surgeon been called?' Sadic asked, relieved to see Sammy's brisk nod of confirmation. 'Great. Phone X-ray, warn them we might need an urgent scan. And find Abby's parents.'

'They just went to the canteen,' the nurse said, soothing a now tearful Abby.

Bleeding was a post-op complication in any operation. Abby would most likely need to return to Theatre to stop the haemorrhage, which might have been slowly grumbling along overnight.

While Sadie labelled the blood tube for the

lab, the curtains around the bed parted to admit a newcomer.

Noting that Abby's blood pressure had improved slightly, Sadie turned to face the surgeon, ready to bring him up to speed.

Instead the floor dropped from under her feet.

It was him. Gorgeous guy from Vienna. The man she'd spent the night with eleven months ago.

Dressed in navy scrubs, his handsome face and the blue eyes he'd passed on to their daughter shrouded in concern, he skidded to a halt across the bed from Sadie.

Their eyes locked for a split second. Awareness she might have imagined zapping across the space, as if their bodies recognised each other, even as their minds played catch-up.

'What's the situation?' he asked, already focussed on their patient, as if Sadie was just any other paediatrician.

Herself jolted into action—there would be time later to discover what he was doing in *her* hospital—Sadie briefly outlined Abby's immediate medical history and the current state of the emergency. In equal parts stunned and elated to see him again, Sadie had no idea how she managed to sound so normal when her own pulse raced dangerously high.

In contrast, the surgeon took charge of the situation in that same calm, confident manner she'd found so attractive that night in Vienna.

As the frantic activity around Abby's bed continued while they all tried to stabilise the girl, Sadie wondered if she'd imagined the moment of shock in his eyes. But focussing on their patient helped Sadie's brain to compute his surreal presence.

He was a doctor. It made sense. She'd met him at a bar close to the hospital.

'Call the lab and get cross-matched blood sent around to Theatre,' he said to Sammy, while he quickly examined Abby's abdomen. 'Now, please.'

'Do you want an urgent scan?' Sadie asked, pulling her phone from her pocket to call the X-ray department.

'No time,' he said, glancing at Sadie's name badge, before unlocking the wheels on his side of Abby's bed. 'I'll scan in Theatre.'

Still acting as if he had no recollection of Sadie at all, no recollection that they'd shared what had been, for Sadie, a life-changing night, he manoeuvred the bed from the bay. 'I'll take her there myself.'

He turned to Sammy. 'Send her parents down to Theatre.' Without a backward glance, he steered Abby's bed from the ward, towards the lifts, leaving as quickly as he'd arrived.

Sadie stood frozen in the centre of the ward, trying to catch her breath as she watched his retreat. Her adrenaline faded, leaving only confusion in its wake. The man she'd thought she would never see again, the man who'd unknowingly fathered their beautiful little girl and literally turned Sadie's world upside down, was here, in London.

Why?

Had he followed her here having somehow discovered her identity?

No, he didn't seem to recognise her at all. He'd probably wiped Sadie and that night from his memory. He clearly hadn't obsessed about her in the same way she'd endlessly wondered about him during the nine months of her pregnancy. And since Milly had arrived, she saw his face every time she looked at their baby daughter.

Sadie's blood ran cold on that last thought. Was he here to confront Sadie because he somehow knew about Milly?

No—those were thoughts of a mind in panic. There would be a perfectly logical explanation for his appearance. As soon as Abby's emergency surgery was over, Sadie would find him and tell him that he'd fathered a daughter.

His words from that night in Vienna returned. *'All that love and relationship stuff is for peo-*

*ple hoping to find the one and start a family.
That's not me...'*

What would he say when she told him about their baby? Would he be angry? Blame Sadie for getting pregnant? Would he want nothing to do with his beautiful infant daughter?

Until she could confront him, Sadie was left to ruminate on her questions with only a sick feeling of dread for company.

Aware of someone joining her, she swallowed down the paranoia gripping her throat. She glanced at Sister Samuels, who had returned to her usual efficient and unflappable self after the emergency, where Sadie felt as if she'd entered a bizarre parallel universe.

'So,' Sammy said with sly grin as the regular ward activity resumed around them, 'now that you've met Dr Ježek, our "eligible doctor", do you think you might change your mind, bid on that auction to date him after all? I told you he was gorgeous.'

Sadie's stomach, already in a tight knot after that frustratingly brief and surreal reunion, took another painful twist.

'I don't think so,' she mumbled, trailing after a chuckling Sammy to resume their ward round, cold realisation dawning.

Her baby daddy was not only here in London, a paediatric surgeon working in Sadie's hospital, he was also about to discover that he'd fathered a little girl during their one passionate night together. And to top everything off, the man who'd assured her that he was unerringly single and couldn't be swayed was the newest hospital hottie, and it was Sadie's job to auction him off for a date with the highest bidder.

She massaged her temples, a headache brewing.

Surely her first day back couldn't get any worse.

CHAPTER THREE

As soon as Roman finished operating on his young patient, Abby, he headed back to Sunshine Ward in search of the woman he'd all but accepted he would never see again.

His mind reeled. She hadn't acknowledged him in any way. Did she want to pretend that he didn't exist?

Fortunately, his shock at seeing her again and the emergency unfolding had precluded conversation earlier. Abby's surgery had given him some breathing space, time to sift through his shambolic thoughts now that his mystery woman had a name.

He'd read her name tag: *Dr Sadie Barnes*.

Sadie. It suited her—playful and sophisticated.

His blood stirred at the idea of a repeat of that unforgettable night, but even if she had given him a second thought after they'd kissed goodbye in Vienna, it didn't mean that he could allow himself to pick up where they'd left off. He was still the same broken man she'd met then. He'd come to London to work, nothing more. One locum position in a series of locum positions that was his life now.

In his eagerness to get this situation—them working in the same hospital for the next month—back under his control, he quickened his pace, his rubber-soled theatre shoes squeaking along the corridor. On entering the ward, he spied Sadie at a computer station.

Despite the warnings he'd recited since they'd come face to face earlier—she'd already spent far too much time in his head since that night— he took a second to enjoy the vision. She was deep in concentration, her profile accentuated by her tied-back dark hair the colour of treacle. She looked good. Better than his well-flexed memories recalled.

The jolt of attraction he'd experienced earlier but had been forced to ignore shocked him anew, as if she'd defibrillated his dormant libido the way she had that night they'd met. Two lonely strangers who'd abandoned the search for love, but were still human, still alive, still capable of connection and passion.

When it came to relationships, nothing had changed for Roman. But a part of him couldn't help the surge of gut-churning excitement as he crossed the ward. He hadn't known it back then, but she would become the first woman since his wife and son had been killed to spark in him a restless kind of energy.

If he'd known her name the next morning, when he'd almost immediately regretted their 'no names, no strings' agreement, he might have been tempted to call, to try and see her again. Of course, the anonymous nature of their night together had heightened the mystery. But just because their careers were another thing they had in common alongside inflammable chemistry and a desire to stay single, the zero-temptation arrangement had been for the best.

'Dr Barnes,' he said, interrupting her study of a chest X-ray on the monitor screen, hoping that a few moments of conversation would break the spell she'd held over him these past eleven months and he could finally put his unprecedented fascination with this woman into perspective.

'Oh!' Sadie startled, her hand flying to her chest where her blouse dipped enticingly between her breasts. 'You made me jump. I…wasn't expecting you.'

Her cheeks flamed and she laughed nervously, flashing him that hesitant smile he'd found so utterly appealing the night they'd flirted their way into bed. She glanced down as if she had no idea how beautiful she was, another trait that, for Roman, fuelled his intrigue.

'I thought you'd still be in Theatre,' she continued, 'but here you are, so soon. Good. Great. I hoped we could talk.'

So she had recognised him. Had been expecting him. And now that he was here, he made her nervous.

This interesting news trampled all over his good intentions to stay immune. And that mouth… How many times had he relived her kisses, her cries, her satisfied smile?

'Sorry to startle you,' he said, still wildly attracted to Sadie Barnes. 'I was hoping we could introduce ourselves properly.'

Earlier when their eyes had met, he'd had to snatch his gaze away. The memories slamming into him had been so visceral, he'd feared his feelings would be obvious to all of their colleagues. Now, struck again by serious Vienna flashbacks, he held out his hand, his palm once more tingling in anticipation. 'Roman Ježek.'

Despite touching her throat in a way that told him their mutual attraction was as fierce as ever, Sadie glanced at his hand as if it might be a live snake. Then she gave it a brief but decisive shake, clearing her throat. 'Sadie Barnes. But you already know my name.'

Beyond the flare of arousal, there was something defensive in her eyes, as if by indulging his natural curiosity, in finally learning the name of his secret lover, he'd broken their one-night rule. But he'd bet his last euro that she'd wondered about him, too. If she'd known his name that night, she'd have cried it out often enough.

'I read your name tag.' He shrugged, unperturbed. 'Since we're colleagues, it made sense to be on first-name terms.'

He opened his mouth to ask how she'd been since they parted that night, but Sadie beat him to it.

'What are you doing in London?' she asked, her chin raised in challenge, her composure obviously recovered enough for her to erect a defensive wall. 'How did you…find me?'

Her aloof tone grated on his eardrums, her accusatory stare tensing his shoulders.

Rather than return to him, her eyes darted around the ward as if she was ashamed to be seen with a man with whom she'd had casual sex, as if she hoped to keep their connection a sordid secret.

Well, Roman was a gentleman; her secret was safe.

'Find you…?' Why was she being so…uptight?

Did she think he'd purposefully hunted her down? Deliberately invaded her work environment like some sort of stalker? Would she prefer if he ignored her now, pretend that he hadn't recognised her? Even if he was into such game-playing, he'd spent the best part of a year trying to master his curiosity for this woman, trying to forget about their night of intense pleasure and honest expectations, a night Sadie clearly regretted.

'How on earth would I find you when, until two hours ago, I hadn't even known your name?' He'd only known the sound of her soft groans when he been inside her and the places to kiss to push her over the edge.

'Right...good point.' She nodded, momentarily appeased. 'Sorry, that came out wrong.'

He concealed a sigh, the excited gallop of his pulse puttering out as disappointment bloomed in its place. 'I would have thought it's obvious what I'm doing here. I work here as a locum pae-diatric surgeon.'

He wasn't about to pounce on her at work.

Admittedly, when he'd first moved to London, he'd occasionally fantasised that he might see the Englishwoman he couldn't forget on the Tube, or in a supermarket. But he'd never once imagined that they would wind up being work colleagues. But despite the way she kept checking him out, her gaze roaming his body, she *did* want to pre-tend that they were strangers, not a couple who shared intense sexual chemistry and knew each other's bodies to an intimate degree.

'I see.' She nodded and looked away. 'Of course. Yes. Right. A locum… Temporary… Good to meet you, Dr Ježek.'

But her weird attitude and regret of their night together—a night that, for him, had been rare and unforgettable—would easily crush his temptation to pick up where they'd left off—problem solved.

Grief had changed him. He felt certain he was no longer capable of a relationship, let alone love. A good thing, then, that, unlike last year when they'd seemed to share more than their cynicism for Valentine's Day, any relationship with Sadie, even a friendly one, now seemed fraught with the complications for which he had no time.

Reining in his enthusiasm, Roman changed the subject. 'I've just finished operating on Abby Swift. Would you like an update?'

He indicated the vacant ward office, pulling professional seniority to help him ignore the involuntary reactions of his body, which, despite his own reservations and Sadie's hot-and-cold reception, was still inordinately pleased to see her again.

'Of course,' Sadie said after a moment's hesitation. 'Good idea. Lots to talk about.'

She hurried into the office as if flustered, pacing as far away from him as the confines of the small room would allow.

Roman gently closed the door, keen now that they had some privacy to reassure Sadie that he hadn't pursued her all the way to London in order to declare he'd fallen madly in love or to propose marriage.

She turned to face him and their eyes locked. A crackle of electricity seemed to spark between them in the silence.

Roman's heart thudded. This was bad. A part of him had known it would be this way if he was ever to see her again. Chemistry as hot as theirs was hard to ignore. And despite her nerves, her embarrassment, she felt it too.

She blinked and a switch seemed to flip. 'So I understand there was some post-op bleeding,' she stated, her tone distant where a moment ago she'd looked as if she might tear off his scrubs and ravish him on the desk. A not unpleasant prospect.

'I saw the results of the scan,' she continued, her hands twisting together. 'Abby was lucky. That could have been much more serious.'

She really was nervous.

Roman concealed his frustration and confusion, feeling as if he'd missed the punchline to a joke. 'Yes—a vascular clip had worked loose. The second surgery went well. Abby is now stable after a unit of blood and should be back on the ward shortly.'

'That's good.' Sadie couldn't quite meet his stare, her arms crossed over her waist, her distraction and evasiveness becoming more pronounced as if he were an uninvited guest at a party that she had to evict.

Obviously she wasn't interested in any sort of personal conversation.

But why so uncomfortable? Was it just the sexual tension or something else?

This Sadie was nothing like the chilled and playful woman he'd met in Vienna. At this rate he wouldn't need to curb his attraction, to keep her at arm's length the way he'd kept everyone since his life had imploded four years ago when a car crash had taken the lives of his wife and son.

She would do the work for him.

Perhaps staying strangers back in Vienna had been serendipity, an escape from becoming ensnared in whatever was going on here.

Except they still needed to find a way to work together.

'Look, Sadie, I know it's a bit awkward,' he said, shoving aside his attraction, 'me turning up like this at your workplace, but, I assure you, it's just a coincidence.'

He paused, hopeful that she might relax, but

if anything being alone with him in this tiny office was making her more nervous.

'Coincidence...' she mumbled and began pacing again. 'It's crazy. What are the chances...?'

He nodded. 'I know, I was shocked to see you this morning. Pleased too. I thought I'd never see you again.'

He smiled his most benign smile while Sadie looked on warily, frowning as if he'd slipped into his native Czech and expected her to understand.

Now that they were away from prying eyes on the ward, it was time to clear the air, reassure her that he was the same man she'd met in Vienna.

'So, how have you been since we last saw each other?' he pressed on, finally acknowledging their one-night stand.

To his alarm, she paled further at his innocent question.

'Good, thank you,' she said a little too briskly. 'I'm very good, you know, busy. Work, life, the usual. Busy, busy, busy.'

She touched the edge of the desk, tapped her index finger there impatiently, as if he was holding her up and she couldn't wait to get away.

Well, he was hearing the message. She might still fancy him, but she wasn't interested in another hook-up.

'I won't keep you,' he said, himself still frustratingly tangled in the threads of their sexual chemistry, but determined to shake off all pretence now he knew where he stood with this changed woman. 'I just thought, seeing as we need to work together, we should, you know, swap a few polite pleasantries. Maybe dispense with the awkwardness. Put the sex behind us.'

The growing horror of her expression gave him no satisfaction.

She squawked out a strangled laugh, her eyes darting to the door at his back. 'Yes, we do need to work together. That's a good point. We're colleagues.'

Except he couldn't bring himself to just…walk away and ignore her as if they'd never been intimate.

Confused that they were now so obviously out of sync, when the night they'd met they'd effortlessly clicked, he ploughed on. 'I was going to ask you if you fancied grabbing a drink one evening after work, but I can sense that you'd rather forget all about that night and pretend it never happened.'

It was as if London Sadie was an entirely different person.

He'd never been one to play games, another reason he'd avoided becoming romantically involved with anyone after losing Karolina. He'd tried to make that clear in Vienna, and he'd thought, wrongly now it seemed, that Sadie was the same. But she was acting evasive, playing her cards very close to her chest.

'A drink…' Sadie blushed, looked down at her feet, chewed ferociously at her lip. 'Oh…um… That was kind of you… A drink…'

Kind of him…? Roman barely held in his snort of disbelief. 'Yes, you know, they sell them in bars and café's as social lubricants.'

'Hmm… I was actually going to suggest the same thing,' she continued, now meeting his eye, 'and then I found out that you're the hospital's "eligible doctor".' She made finger quotes. 'So, you know, a drink probably isn't the best idea…' She waved her hand vaguely. 'And as we've just established, I'm a registrar and you're a consultant, so we probably shouldn't, you know, socialise or tongues will start wagging.'

Was she filling the awkward silence? Waffling out of nervousness? Surely she would soon run out of excuses.

'And I work late most nights,' she rushed on, 'as I'm sure do you, with all of your operating and stuff, so that doesn't leave a lot of time for a drink, anyway…'

Roman tuned out, marvelling that she had barely paused for breath, her vocalised stream of consciousness obviously a nervous gesture and, to Roman's ears, one big let-down.

Her cheeks were growing pinker by the second. 'And my sister is staying with me at the moment, off and on, and—'

He held up his hand, stopping her mid-flow. 'Don't worry. You don't need to add that you're busy watching paint dry. I get it. You're really not interested in clearing the air, or being friendly.'

She flicked her ponytail over her shoulder. 'I—'

'Look,' he interrupted what would likely be another raft of excuses, 'just to reassure you, I didn't stalk you for eleven months, nor did I seek out a job here just so I could swear undying love.'

She snorted, her expression horrified, as if she had no understanding that he was joking.

'Yes, I thought we had a good time in Vienna,' he continued, 'at least it seemed that way to me, unless you were faking it. And given that we've seen each other naked and now have to work together until I leave in a few weeks, I hoped we could be mature and respectful, even friends.' He shrugged, knowing that the chemistry would pose a big barrier to that. 'But you don't have to make excuses. A *no* is sufficient. I'm a grown-up. I assure you, I'll be fine.'

He stepped back, giving her more space and preparing to draw a line under this puzzling reunion. Roman shook his head, defeated.

Where had that passionate woman gone? They almost hadn't made it inside her Vienna hotel room, their heated kisses spilling over from the lift into the deserted corridor while they'd fumbled with the room's lock. She'd been as insatiable for him as he'd been for her. They'd had sex not once, but twice.

But where that unguarded part of Roman only she had managed to sneak past had seen this chance meeting as a gift, an opportunity to once more explore the undeniable chemistry they'd discovered in Vienna, for Sadie, one night had obviously been enough.

'Hold on,' she said, frowning, jabbing a finger in his direction. 'A: I faked nothing and B: Don't try and make me out to be the bad guy here. You're the one who volunteered to date a woman for the Valentine's fundraiser.'

At his gobsmacked confusion, she clarified.

'*I'm* the person who's been chosen to auction you off like a prize stud. What happened to *Mr I'm Not Looking for a Relationship*? If what you told me in Vienna is true, don't you think you're misleading all those potential bidders who think they stand a chance with you? Not to mention that you're happy to be the fundraiser's eligible poster boy and then inviting me out for a drink. That wasn't the man I met in Vienna, unless your whole "not looking for love" thing was a charade. Who's fake now, huh?'

Roman frowned, trying to decipher if she was mad that he'd tricked her, jealous that he was expected to take the auction winner out to dinner, or indifferent beyond ensuring that the auction was accurately represented.

'*You're* accusing *me* of lying?' he said, stunned. He'd been honest that night. He wasn't the man for someone looking for a relationship, not even a casual one. 'Because if you want to talk about deceptions, I can't even believe that you're the same woman I met then.'

They faced each other, breaths gusting in mutual outrage. Any trace of the common ground they'd shared that night seemed long gone.

'Look.' He sighed, scrubbing a hand through his hair. 'I didn't lie to you in Vienna, and, yes, I did volunteer for the auction.'

Allow himself to be coerced, more like. He hadn't wanted to participate in the stupid fundraiser at all. But the formidable Sister Samuels wouldn't take no for an answer. And the part of him still wondering about his mysterious Valentine's lover had needed to forget about her, to accept that he was never going to see her again. Volunteering for a good cause had seemed like a painless way to close that chapter, once and for all.

But she needn't worry. He'd meant what he'd said last Valentine's Day. Love, romance, relationships were mostly for people looking for commitment and family in their future, and Roman had already found and lost more than many people experienced in a lifetime.

'Exactly,' she said triumphantly, aiming her index finger at the centre of his chest as if her point were spectacularly proved.

Recalling the lengths he'd gone to to make Sadie understand he was unavailable in Vienna and realising it now looked as if he were actively seeking a partner, he rushed to offer reassurance. 'It's just a fundraiser for a good cause. I'm not interested in relationships, the whole "marriage and kids" thing, I can assure you. Everything I said to you that night still stands.'

He was still the loner she'd met at an Anti-Valentine's party, still trying to outrun his grief and loneliness. Still trying to forget that he'd taken his once full and happy life for granted until it was destroyed by a drunk driver one rainy night.

Maybe if she realised that he was the same person she'd slept with because they were both safe from emotional entanglement, she could relax. He wanted a casual drink, the odd polite hello, not a lifelong commitment. Maybe then, they could get back to the light-hearted vibe of their first conversation, because this one wasn't going at all the way he'd planned.

Sadie seemed lost for words, so he continued, 'I'm simply going along with "a date"—' now it was his turn to make finger quotes '—to help raise funds for the hospital.'

Making polite conversation over a one-off dinner was one thing, but he wasn't the man of anyone's dreams. 'I'm not even going to be in London that long. I'll be leaving in a few weeks for my next locum position in Ireland. The entire reason I locum is because I'm not interested in putting down any roots. What's that expression? A rolling stone gathers no moss.'

Rather than look appeased, Sadie seemed to turn a shade paler, swallowing as if her throat was dry. 'No roots... Good. That's good news. Excellent.'

Her mouth formed a bright, clearly fake smile and she brushed a speck from her blouse. 'Because I'm not sure it's a good look for the hospital's eligible doctor to go gadding about with other women when a date with you is the fundraiser's most anticipated auction. The current family room and playroom are in desperate need of a makeover,' she added primly, 'and I want to help make the auction a big success and bring in as much money as possible...'

She was doing it again, barely pausing for

breath. One vague excuse after another. He mentally scratched his head at her evasiveness. He'd never met anyone so hard to pin down to a straight answer. Emotionally, this Sadie gave nothing away.

'No one is going to bid for a date with you,' she continued, as if flustered by the idea, 'if they see you out and about with every single woman you can lay your hands on. And on that note, you'll probably need to try and be a little more charming on the night of the auction, perhaps don't lead with the whole "anti-commitment" speech thing.' More finger quotes. 'We don't want to dissuade the bidders…'

Finally, she ran out of steam. She raised her chin defiantly, her pretty eyes flashing.

'What on earth is gadding?' he said, his lips twitching, certain that he'd never done it but intrigued anew by her jealousy. There was still a part of her that didn't want to see him take out another woman.

More mixed messages.

Just then her pager sounded. She checked the screen, her body visibly sagging as if she was relieved to have a reason to get away from him at last.

'I'm afraid you'll have to figure that out on your own,' she said, moving past him and reaching for the door handle. 'I have a patient to discharge, so you'll have to excuse me.'

Had they resolved a single thing?

'Of course.' Roman stepped aside, struggling to reconcile the dismissal and confusion with their obviously mutual and ongoing chemistry.

Some women he'd had casual sex with became clingy, as if they hoped they could change him, even though he was always as honest as he'd been with Sadie. His commitment avoidance wasn't a lifestyle choice; it was self-preservation for a man who'd lost everything he'd loved.

But *this* woman was acting as if she wanted nothing more than to return to being strangers.

She tugged at the handle with force, clearly hoping to make a grand exit so that he knew exactly where he stood.

Except the door didn't budge.

She tugged again, a soft grunt of frustration leaving her lips.

Roman hid a smile. Despite their ridiculous disagreement, which for the life of him he couldn't even decide what it had been about, she intrigued him, even when she was upset.

Flustered, Sadie gripped the door handle with both hands, her knuckles white as if escape had become a matter of life or death. She blew wisps of hair from her eyes as she jiggled the handle with enough force to yank the fixing screws from the wood.

She was so close, he could detect her perfume. It brought a fleeting vision of him spinning her around, pressing her back against the door and kissing her thoroughly until this confusing interlude, her blowing hot and cold, made sense.

Not that he would ever do such a thing.

She'd made it clear: they were done.

So much for the fantasies that had crept under his guard, fantasies where they'd gone for that drink, continued to discover how much more they had in common beyond rampant attraction and resumed their casual fling for the weeks he had left in London.

'Allow me to try,' he said, when she continued to battle fruitlessly with the door.

'Fine,' she said with a huff, relinquishing the handle and stepping aside.

But the room's large desk prevented her moving too far.

He gripped the cool metal door handle, aware that they now shared a bubble of close personal space. He waited, poised for the absurdity of their unnecessary confrontation and them being trapped in an office together to trigger the laughter that had once come so easily and spontaneously while they'd flirted.

He looked down and she looked up, their eyes clashing.

Every erotic memory from that night came rushing back.

Her scent triggered olfactory reminders of how he'd left her room that night with her perfume lingering on his skin.

Her lips parted on a barely audible gasp, her breath gusting as they stared, locked together in the charged moment of stalemate. She blinked up at him, breathing hard.

Roman glanced at her mouth, recalled that first heady taste of their kiss.

His invitation to a drink hovered on his lips once more.

No; it was over.

The handle gave way under his hand, the door swinging gently open without a hitch.

He deflated, the moment gone. 'After you.'

'Thank you,' she said, averting her stare, hurrying onto the ward.

Roman stared at her retreat, the restlessness back.

Yes, she'd been the only woman to worm her way inside his mind and set up camp since his wife, but they were destined to be nothing more to each other than polite strangers who worked together.

He'd allowed himself a brief reprieve from his

solitude that night in her arms, but now he'd have to ignore the sparks and steer clear of her for a few weeks. The Sadie of his daydreams and the Sadie of reality were two completely different women. Neither of them wanted anything to do with him, and that should suit him just fine.

CHAPTER FOUR

LATER THAT AFTERNOON, Sadie flashed her hospital security tag at the theatre receptionist, her stomach a tight ball of nerves and nausea.

How had she managed to botch her interaction with Roman so spectacularly? Before she'd discovered from Sammy that her mystery lover was the hospital hottie being auctioned for a date, everything had been so clear in her head.

Her plan had been simple: express surprise that he was in London, suggest a meeting outside work so they could talk in private and then casually inform him that their night of passion had created a miracle little girl with his blue eyes and Sadie's smile.

Easy.

In her fantasy version of the conversation, he would have expressed delight at the news and understanding that she'd had no way of contacting him after their no-strings hook-up. They might have laughed at the foolishness of sleeping with an anonymous stranger and praised their good luck that fate had once more thrown them together. Roman would see how much Sadie loved Milly, certainly enough for two parents, and they would work together for a few weeks and then part as friends when he left London.

Only nothing about the conversation on Sunshine Ward had worked out the way Sadie had planned. Firstly, she'd been terrified that Sammy or some other keen-eyed nurse would see them together, put two and two together and figure out that he was Milly's father, before she'd had a chance to tell him. Then she'd been struck tongue-tied by the claustrophobic closeness of him in that tiny office, his imposing height and muscular strength reminding her how hard he'd clung to her as he'd groaned into her neck when they'd been intimate. While she'd been dealing with the roar of renewed attraction—he was impossibly and unfairly even hotter than eleven months earlier—and the unexpected shafts of jealousy that she had to fix him up with some other woman, she'd become horribly flustered, dithering and mumbling her way through a list of excuses the length of her arm.

Initially, she'd been hurt when she'd assumed he'd lied to her about wanting to stay single in Vienna. Then he'd made it glaringly clear that he still wasn't interested in a family, even clarifying the ground rules while inviting her for a drink as if he expected that they could pick up where they'd left off physically.

Great casual sex? Yes!

A relationship...a family? No way!

He was a loner. A rolling stone. The fact that she still fancied him was irrelevant.

No wonder she'd utterly fumbled her calm and rational plan to tell him her big, life-changing news. News that might ruin any chance of the amicable working relationship he suggested. She'd over-talked, weighed down by the pressure of what she had to confess, of finding the right time, and saying the right things so he understood that, when it came to raising their daughter, she required nothing from him, neither emotionally nor financially. She just needed him to know of Milly's existence.

Resolved to pull herself together and carry out her mission, properly this time, she pushed through the double doors in search of the theatre staff room. She hoped to catch him between surgeries, and before she headed home to Milly. No matter how much or little he wanted to be part of his daughter's life, he deserved to know that he was a father.

As she rounded the staffroom doorway, distracted by the enormity of what she needed to confess, and wary of his possible reactions given their disastrous meeting earlier, she smacked head first into an impressive wall of maleness.

The breath whooshed from her lungs.

Firm hands gripped her upper arms.

Awash in the heady scent of subtly sexy after-shave, Sadie looked up, meeting the piercing blue gaze of the man himself.

Roman Ježek. She couldn't get used to how sensual his name sounded.

'Sorry,' she mumbled, determined to ignore how hot he looked in his scrubs by keeping her eyes on his this time.

Except her reason for being there dissolved in the face of how horribly attracted to him she still found herself. All she could recall was that he'd wanted to take her out for a drink and how, for a thrilling, irrational second, he'd looked as if he might kiss her when she'd struggled to open the office door.

No, those thoughts were banned.

Expecting some short retort, she glanced at his mouth, which was compressed with annoyance. Big mistake. He was close enough to kiss. He was a phenomenal kisser. She hadn't been kissed by anyone since him, that restrained and tender goodbye kiss they'd shared the fodder for all of her fantasies these past eleven months.

'Are you okay?' he asked, ducking his head

to peer into her face with his intuitive-seeming concern.

She nodded as her heart banged against her ribs so hard he must be able to feel it, given she was plastered to his hard chest the way she'd been when they were naked and lost in baby-making passion.

Why didn't he push her away? Why couldn't she find the strength to move?

'Fine… I'm fine,' she muttered, not trusting herself to say anything more sophisticated in case she blurted out the truth about their baby in an emotion-fuelled rush.

But it wasn't fair for him to find out that he was a father in a busy corridor outside a crowded staff room when he still had to spend the afternoon operating.

'I… I came to find you,' she said, wincing at how pathetic she sounded.

With Roman once more up close, irrelevant and pointless memories of Roman the lover blasted her body like mini electric shocks. The way he'd held her face when he'd kissed her lips. The intensity of his passion, as if he hadn't been intimate with anyone in a long time. The split second of regret she'd noticed in his eyes when he'd kissed her goodbye.

While their baby had grown inside her, she'd imagined scenarios like this, where they somehow met once more, their chemistry still off the charts.

Except Sadie knew from experience how reality crushed dreams. And she had bigger problems than erasing Roman Ježek from her erotic fantasies. Like how, flustered earlier, she'd offended him, as good as accusing him of stalking, and now needed to apologise. Like how, despite the way he'd looked at her when he'd asked her how she'd been, she had to set him up on a date with some other horny woman. Like how a man with his gifts—handsome, intelligent, confident, willing to play the prize stud in a Valentine's Day auction—most likely had a string of casual conquests littered across Europe.

And don't forget darling Milly…

'Why *did* you come to find me?' he asked, finally releasing her from his grip and folding his arms across his broad chest. 'I thought we said everything we needed to say earlier.'

Why was she here…?

Oh, yes!

'We did say…a lot, but I need to ask you something.'

There was so much more to say. But now that the time had come to apologise, to invite him for that drink *he'd* suggested and subtly slip into conversation that, against all odds, they'd created a life together, her mind had gone blank.

'I'm listening,' he said.

What was it about this man that turned her brain to mush and her body to molten need?

Stepping back, she mentally reprimanded her foolish libido. No matter what fantasies she'd harboured of a repeat performance of Vienna—the best sex of her life— Roman was a self-confessed commitment-phobe who would likely scarper abroad as quickly as his theatre shoes could carry him once she told him about Milly.

'I'm not interested in relationships, the whole "marriage and kids" thing... I'm not interested in putting down any roots...'

Determined that this time there would be no nervous verbal diarrhoea, she cleared her throat, her composure ragged. 'I've thought about it, and I think your idea of meeting for a drink is a good one.'

She sagged with relief, her message successfully delivered.

'Really?' he said, his expression sceptical, all trace of this morning's even-tempered and friendly Roman gone.

She hadn't planned for his refusal.

Before she could explain, utter one word of her apology, a nurse left the staffroom, squeezing past Sadie and Roman, who were still partly obscuring the doorway, shoving them once more almost chest to chest.

'What about your busy schedule and your list of excuses, and the fact that I'm to be auctioned off like a prize bull?' he said seemingly completely unfazed by their proximity, where she was struggling to forget how it had felt to be naked and crushed in his arms.

Sadie winced, looked away from the sexy peek of dark chest hair at the V-neck of his scrubs, regretting that her earlier dithering had armed him with ammunition to mount a counter-attack.

'I did make excuses,' she said, wishing she could just blurt out her announcement and then run. But this busy hospital corridor wasn't the right environment for the serious conversation required. Although she was struggling to come up with an appropriate venue to tell someone they'd unknowingly fathered a child...

Her flat was packed to the rafters with baby paraphernalia. She couldn't just invite herself to his place. It would have to be a café or a pub.

'I'm sorry about that,' she added, stepping aside so they no longer obstructed the doorway. 'I was just a little thrown by seeing you at my hospital, appearing like a genie from a lamp, looking...' she waved her hand in his general direction '...heart-attack gorgeous in scrubs.'

He leaned one shoulder against the wall in a relaxed slouch, a smile playing around his mouth. 'Gorgeous, eh?'

Sadie flushed and his stare softened slightly, although Sadie might have imagined his empathy, because he continued, 'But you think it's inappropriate for us to socialise, so why your sudden change of heart?'

Despite his justified objections—she had made him sweat earlier—he infuriatingly tilted his head in that distracting way she remembered from Vienna when he'd been playful and flirtatious and seductive, the look in his eyes doing things to her body she'd thought were impossible after the physical ordeals of pregnancy and birth and the fatigue of new motherhood.

Sadie chewed her lip, wishing that she'd prepared better for both his up-close hotness and his understandable resistance.

'You said it yourself.' She shrugged, hoping he couldn't sense her desperation. 'We're colleagues.'

Sadie wasn't ready to be completely honest and vulnerable with this cool and aloof version of Roman. It would be hard enough to tell him that they'd made a baby together.

Instead she smiled sweetly. 'It makes sense for us to clear the air, after…you know.'

She whispered the last two words, heat scalding her neck. She didn't want to talk about the amazing sex where they could be overheard by other hospital staff. She didn't even want to think about the amazing sex given there was now no chance of a repeat. But all she could think about was the amazing sex and how it would be criminal to waste the opportunity to see if it was just as good a second time.

The seconds ticked while he watched her with narrowed eyes.

The longer they stood here arguing, the greater the risk that she would be spotted by someone she knew, someone who might ask after the baby.

His baby!

The last thing she wanted was for him to find out about their daughter inadvertently.

'So, are you in or out?' She backed up towards the exit, trying to keep the emotional maelstrom taking place inside from her expression. She was close to begging, fearful of his eventual reaction and desperate to escape his magnetism, which only seemed to be growing stronger the more time they spent together.

Her rampant hormones were torturous. And her tingling breasts told her that she needed to get home to feed Milly.

Roman held up his hands in supplication, stepping closer so they wouldn't be overheard.

'Look, Sadie, I'm a simple man. I'm just here to do my job for the next three and a half weeks, and then I'll be moving on. I don't want to get involved in anything…complicated. I thought you understood that in Vienna.'

Sadie forced the frozen smile to remain on her face, aware that what he wanted—no strings, no ties, no roots—was irrelevant. A child was the ultimate in complications. He might be the same man she'd met in Vienna with the same priorities, but for Sadie, everything had changed since then, for the better.

But his reminder of his footloose and fancy-free attitude mocked her for the idiotic fantasies she'd indulged since seeing him again. Her hope that they might once more become temporary lovers, or find an amicable way to co-parent, shredded like sodden paper. She should have known not to trust her instincts when it came to men. Mark's cruel betrayal had taught her that valuable lesson.

A dull throb pounded at her temples.

'So you need to make up your mind,' he continued, his arms crossed, 'to be sure of what you want. Because I'm not into playing games.'

'I am sure,' Sadie said, growing increasingly frantic inside. If she'd agreed to go for a drink when *he'd* issued the invitation, she wouldn't need to grovel now. 'I just want us to talk, in private, away from the hospital.'

This was ridiculous. She was practically begging him to meet her for a purely platonic drink, when in reality she still wanted to tear his clothes off and could do no such thing.

The universe clearly hated her…

Still he made her suffer, his expression unconvinced. 'I'll be honest—you seem like a completely different woman from the one I met in Vienna. Evasive, hard to pin down, uncertain of what you want…'

Sadie gaped, horrified that he saw her most telling traits so clearly. But she *was* different. She was a mother now. To *his* daughter.

'I'm the same person, just a year older and wiser.' She hadn't lied to him that night, either. Yes, their chemistry fried her brain, but she wasn't looking for a relationship either.

He frowned. 'Earlier on the ward,' he said in that low, calm voice that was starting to irk her, 'I sensed some…what's the word in English…?' He glanced at the ceiling while he searched his vocabulary then clicked his fingers as he found the right word. 'Hostility from you.'

Sadie's jaw dropped. 'Hostility?'

He nodded, inflaming her further. 'I thought we could behave like adults, but one minute you're dismissing my invitation, the next changing your mind.'

'I was not being hostile. I think the word you actually mean is "circumspection". I was being respectful of our working relationship.'

But of course, she had dismissed him, out of fear and nerves and sheer panic, everything all at once conspiring to throw her into a state where all she'd been able to offer were blabbered excuses.

He stared, his lips twitching with amusement. 'I'll look up the meaning of that one while I'm also looking up "gadding".'

Sadie tried to stay aloof with him, but the absurdity of their bickering finally registered and she laughed it off with a shake of her head.

When she looked up he was smiling.

'So, will you meet me for a drink or not?' she asked, dragging in a shuddering breath, because this Roman was the man she'd flirted with in Vienna. A straight-up, say-it-like-it-is, intelligent and funny guy who would surely react positively to the news that he had a daughter.

Wouldn't he…?

But what if, for him, Milly wasn't wanted, even though for Sadie their daughter was a treasured miracle?

Well, if that was the case, it would be his loss. His disappearance from their lives would even be convenient, given that Sadie couldn't seem to switch off her attraction to the exasperating man.

He inched closer, his smile fading. 'How could I refuse such a romantic invitation?'

He looked up from staring at her mouth and their eyes met.

Sadie held her breath, trapped in his magnetic

force field the way she'd been when she'd lost her battle with the stubborn office door earlier.

'Thank you.' With trembling fingers, she took a piece of paper from her pocket and thrust it his way. 'Here's my number. There's a bar not far from here. I won't be at work tomorrow, so text me what night works for you.'

With a nod and an inscrutable look, he slid the piece of paper into the breast pocket of his scrubs.

Just then, a surgical technician appeared and interrupted them so they moved apart, once more at a respectable distance.

'We're ready for you, Doc,' the man said to Roman.

'I'll text you,' he said to Sadie, the intense and searching look he shot her before walking away setting off another cascade of hormones that left her weak-kneed and emotionally drained.

She waited until he was out of sight before she sagged against the wall, exhausted, all her adrenaline used up. This infatuation was bad. Worse than she'd expected. Because no matter how rampant their persistent chemistry, she needed to see him as a colleague, and a co-parent and nothing more. No lusting, no kissing and, categorically, no more amazing sex.

CHAPTER FIVE

THE FOLLOWING EVENING, Roman stood as Sadie walked into the small, intimate bar not far from the hospital. His nerves buzzed with excitement. She looked sensational in black jeans and a red top, with silver hoops in her ears.

Brushing a hand down the front of his freshly pressed shirt, he stepped forward to greet her, reminding himself that this wasn't a date even if they had dressed up for each other. Except his eyes moved over her figure, reacquainting themselves with her pert breasts, her slim waist and the tantalising curve of her hips.

He released a silent groan of frustration, relieved when she spied him, her smile that hesitant one he found so intriguing. Her approving gaze gave him a similar once-over as she walked his way.

It was still there, the undeniable chemistry that had driven them from strangers to lovers.

'Hi. You look gorgeous,' he said, using the

term she'd applied to him yesterday, outside the theatre staff room.

He pressed a kiss to her cheek, catching the scent of her shampoo, briefly closing his eyes against the flood of erotic memories he would need to crush, and fast.

'Thank you,' she said as he pulled out her chair before taking the seat opposite. A hint of wariness lingered in her expression; like him, she was nervous. 'Thanks for coming.'

'No problem.' He'd made a decision on the way to the bar: he intended to explain to Sadie why he didn't date beyond casually, why he needed to keep constantly moving, why he could never be truly *eligible*.

His story wouldn't be pretty, but would hopefully put Sadie's mind at ease once and for all, manage expectations between them so they could focus on being friendly colleagues.

Colleagues who needed a fire extinguisher to douse the flames of their chemistry.

The waiter appeared and took their drinks order and then left again.

For a moment, they faced each other in silence across the table for two near the window that Roman had chosen for privacy. It was as if this drink represented a fresh start, and neither of them wanted to put a foot wrong after yesterday's misunderstandings.

'I'm sorry—'

'I wanted to apologise—'

They spoke over each other and then laughed, the tension easing.

'After you,' he said, resting his forearms on the table and watching her across the flickering flame of a candle in a jar.

'I wanted to apologise for yesterday,' she said, glancing down. 'I was totally thrown by seeing you again, especially at work.'

Roman nodded, entranced by the way she toyed with her hair, which tonight was an exhilarating tumble of soft waves he wanted to cup to his face and inhale.

'Me too. I understand and I'm glad we're being honest. If only we'd talked about our jobs that night in Vienna. I was a locum at the hospital.'

Sadie smiled, rolling her eyes at their foolishness. 'And I'd attended the Progress in Paediatrics conference that day.'

Roman relaxed. The easy-going, animated Sadie was back, and the sight of her laced his blood with endorphins.

But he couldn't allow the sparkle in her eyes when she smiled to distract him from his purpose. 'Listen, Sadie, I feel like I owe you an explanation—I wasn't entirely open with you that day we met.'

Sadie waved her hand, began shaking her head

as if to shut down his apology, but he needed to lay all his cards on the table so they could move on as colleagues. The sexual attraction would fade and, if it didn't, the physical distance of his next locum position in Ireland would finally cure his obsession.

'Please let me say this,' he pleaded.

She stilled, her stare wary once more.

'I don't tell everyone I meet my whole story,' he said, dragging in a shuddering breath, steeling himself as he always needed to in order to speak about his loss, 'but with you, I think it's relevant and I want you to know.'

Stricken, she flushed. 'Roman, you don't owe me any explanations. In fact, I have something—'

He held up his hand, cutting her off. 'I want to explain. Please let me. Hopefully you'll understand me a little better.'

'Okay,' she said in a small voice.

The waiter returned with their drinks, the pause giving Roman a few seconds to prepare. No matter how painful to relive, he hoped his confession would finally settle any awkwardness between him and Sadie. She would see that he was the same man she met in Vienna, that he wasn't romantically pursuing her or anyone else.

That he would always be content to spend Valentine's Days alone.

'I was married once,' he said when the waiter

had walked away. He braced for the familiar dull ache in his chest, which varied in intensity depending on how occupied he kept his mind, but never fully disappeared and likely never would.

'Oh…okay,' Sadie said, subdued, glancing down at the flickering candle in the centre of their table.

'My wife died four years ago,' Roman added, keen to have his part of the conversation over with, as if spewing out the words would lessen their devastating impact.

She looked up. 'I'm so sorry,' she whispered, horror and compassion in her stare.

Roman shook his head, trying to recall the last time he'd opened up to someone. 'Since then, I've been a bit of a loner—the man you met that night where we were both avoiding Valentine's Day.'

Her hand covered his on the table between them, instinctively offering comfort.

His body jolted at her touch, the jarring juxtaposition between grief and arousal.

'I wanted to explain,' he continued, relieved to see she understood, 'how I might be game for a one-off dinner date to raise money for a good cause that helps sick children, but I'm not, and never will be, relationship material.'

She started blinking, her frown deepening. 'You're grieving,' she said as if to herself, moisture shining in her eyes. 'Really, you don't have to explain further.'

She looked crestfallen, more devastated than he'd expected. Sadie certainly wore her heart on her sleeve. He'd seen glimpses of her compassion for her patients on the ward, where she was a favourite with the kids. But to have that compassion directed his way left him unsettled, a return of the restless energy he'd experienced the night they met.

'I know, but there's more.' He rubbed a hand over his clean-shaven jaw, sucking in another fortifying breath, confiding in her easy.

'Okay.' Sadie nodded, her eyes round with trepidation.

Roman forced out the words a big part of him still struggled to believe could be true. 'I also had a six-year-old son. He was with my wife in the car the night of the accident. They died together.'

Shock drained the colour from Sadie's face, one hand squeezing his and her other hand coming up to cover her mouth. 'Oh, my goodness. I'm so sorry, Roman. I don't even know what to say.' Tears filled her eyes. She looked bereft.

Roman turned his hand over under hers, palm to palm, the gesture natural after their other intimacies. 'No need to say anything.'

He smiled a sad smile, not bothering to hide

his feelings from this empathetic woman with whom he'd found a surprising connection.

But now she knew his darkest moment.

As she stared into his eyes, Sadie swallowed, visibly struggling to regain her composure.

'I just wanted to be straight up with you,' he continued, 'to avoid any more misunderstandings. Of course, you're more than a work colleague, although we're putting our physical relationship behind us.'

She looked away, but not before he witnessed her disappointment.

He too felt the stomach-sinking emptiness. He would struggle to ignore their chemistry. Aside from fierce attraction, he liked and respected Sadie. Opening up to her felt good, brought them closer.

'So now you know; I'm not a stalker or a liar or a player. Why we had so much in common last year, wanting nothing to do with Valentine's Day.' He smiled, worried that his news seemed to have hit Sadie hard.

That she was so affected by his story touched him, but now he wanted to lighten the mood.

'Of course, I feel the same this year, but what can I say…? I found it very hard to say no to Sammy about the auction. She twisted my arm the first day I arrived.'

'Yes…that does explain…everything.' She'd

turned pale, seemed agitated, shifting in her chair and tugging at the neck of her sweater.

'We don't have to talk about it if you'd rather not, but how do you even begin to deal with something like that?' she asked, her voice a bewildered whisper.

'Staying away from the memories of my family life in Prague helps,' he admitted. 'That's why locum work suits me. I keep moving, keep my life simple—work, sleep, repeat.'

'A rolling stone,' she said, frowning, glancing down at their still-clasped hands.

As if self-conscious that they'd comforted each other in a moment of vulnerability, she slid her hand from his and took a shaky sip of her drink.

'Thanks for listening,' he said, hoping to draw a line under the subject while trying not to focus on how cold his hand was without her touch. 'I hope now we can work together for the next few weeks without any…awkwardness.'

Who knew, maybe they could even be friends? Although how he was going to switch off his attraction to her, he had no clue.

She nodded, forcing a smile that didn't reach her eyes, sat up straighter. 'Absolutely. That's what I want, too. Good. Great.'

She didn't sound certain. She sounded distant again.

'I'm sorry. My turn to do the listening,' he said,

recalling how she'd invited him for this drink. 'I interrupted you earlier. You wanted to talk about something?'

He smiled, encouragingly.

She gave a nervous laugh and couldn't meet his eyes.

His stomach sank. It made no sense. He'd been honest. Cleared the air. Sadie's bouts of evasiveness brought out his need for control. He'd deliberately kept his life simple these past four years—a coping mechanism. But now he wondered if, physical compatibility aside, he and Sadie would ever again be on the same wavelength.

Sadie's heart was beating so fast she feared she might pass out, collapse face first onto the candle and singe her hair. But after Roman's tragic revelation, even that humiliating scenario would be preferable to confessing the real reason she'd invited him there tonight.

How could she tell him about Milly when her news would surely heighten the grief she saw so clearly in his tortured eyes?

He'd lost the people he'd loved the most. Her chest ached from watching him paste on a brave face. She couldn't cause him any more pain. Sadie's revelation should be joyous and optimistic, not shrouded in the understandably heartbreaking sadness of this moment.

But would there ever be an appropriate time to break the news that he was already a father again, when he had such compelling reasons to avoid being in that vulnerable position?

Offering him what felt like a watery smile, Sadie trawled her stunned mind for a substitute topic of conversation.

'I…um…actually wanted to ask you some background questions,' she said, frantically improvising by taking out her phone. 'You know, for the fundraiser. I have to write up a biography for your auction, something to get the bidding started. Is that okay?'

The fundraiser. It seemed so trivial now.

'Of course.' Roman shrugged in that laidback way of his, levelling his unwavering gaze on Sadie.

She blinked away the sting of tears, still haunted by Roman's grief and by what it meant for his relationship with his daughter.

Ever since he'd strode onto Sunshine Ward, Sadie had indulged fantasies of the kind of father he'd make, the kind of relationship he'd have with their baby. Only, considering what she'd just learned, there was no guarantee that he'd want anything to do with Milly and, worse, a part of Sadie would understand why.

How devastating to lose your only child and your partner in the same tragic event. As a new mother, Sadie could only imagine the heartache he'd endured, every parent's worst nightmare. He hadn't blithely sworn off relationships and family to enjoy his life free of responsibilities, as she'd assumed. He'd closed himself off to emotional entanglements as a defence mechanism.

That she definitely understood.

Focussed on her phone, Sadie opened the notes app. 'So what made you choose a career in Paediatrics?' she asked, pretending to read from a list of prepared questions.

The way he was looking at her, as if his intense stare might be able to read all her secrets, was not only terrifying, it was also leaving her hot and bothered.

How could she possibly be any more attracted to this man?

Except he'd opened up to her, trusted her with his deepest wound. Her hormones were running amok.

'My uncle is a surgeon in the Czech Republic,' he said with fondness in his eyes. 'Growing up, I knew that I wanted to help people. While I was training to be a surgeon I completed a post in paediatric surgery and I loved it.'

His expression became animated. It took a special kind of person to work with sick children.

But there must be moments when his work reminded him of his own son. It showed his already impressive dedication and compassion in a whole new and utterly appealing light.

'I like the variety of the work,' he continued, the spark in his eyes mesmerising, 'which is much like the old adult general surgical position that is now becoming obsolete as sub-specialisation grows.'

Sadie nodded, making brief notes on her phone, while every word he spoke embedded in her memory and set her nervous system aflutter. His commitment to paediatrics was seriously compelling and a massive turn-on.

No matter how hard she hoped, their chemistry wasn't going to just evaporate.

If only there were a way to move past it so she could focus on introducing Roman to Milly. If only it were as simple as resuming a casual fling to get each other out of their systems. But how could she allow herself to embrace the passion she felt simmering below the surface when she still needed to tell him her big secret?

She was trapped in limbo, wanting him but needing to stay objective.

'And the locum work also provides plenty of variety,' she said, unsurprised now that he needed to outrun such painful memories by keeping on the move.

The idea of him leaving London, of never seeing him again, hollowed out her stomach for both herself and Milly. Sadie and Grace had a close relationship with both their parents. She'd wanted the same for Milly.

But Roman had no intention of putting down family roots again, and she couldn't blame him.

'Until four years ago,' he continued speaking while Sadie tried to come to terms with the flood of her emotions, 'I'd never considered leaving Prague. I was lucky.' The haunted look returned to his stare, and Sadie wished she'd been more careful with her questions.

'I had it all,' he said. 'A job I loved. A loving relationship. A family...'

Then his world had collapsed, a devastating loss from which he might never heal. No wonder he wasn't looking for love; he'd already found it, was as emotionally unavailable as it came.

A crack split her heart. Her beloved baby might never get the chance to know this good man. His rejection of her precious Milly would sting, no matter how much Sadie understood Roman's motivation.

Painful memories flashed in her head—her devastating diagnosis, the years of yearning for a child, Mark lobbing blows, one after the other. *It's over. I've found someone else. She's pregnant.*

'What about you?' he asked, blind to Sadie's inner turmoil and feelings of inadequacy, which were shaking her like a rag doll. 'Did you always want to work with children?'

Sadie looked away, terrified that he'd see the knowledge of his daughter lurking in her eyes. A part of her, that maternal instinct, wanted to fight for Milly, to stand up and say, *I feel your pain, but you have a beautiful daughter who deserves to have a father.*

'Not really. I always wanted to be a doctor.' Sadie cleared her throat, torn between understanding for Roman's defence mechanisms, and heartache for their innocent baby, who to Sadie had been only a source of extreme joy.

Except it was too late; Milly was already here.

'I never really thought much about children,' she continued, lured by Roman's honesty to lower the guard she'd had in place since her fertility issues and Mark's cruel betrayal had left her doubting she'd ever again be good enough for a relationship, 'until I was told that I might never be able to have any of my own.'

Now it was his turn to be shocked, his turn to take *her* hand.

They really needed to stop touching each other.

'Then children became all I could think about,' she said in a rush, her history of infertility all tangled up with her omissions about their miracle daughter.

Offering Roman a sad, ironic laugh, she relived the years spent managing the pain of her diagnosis by refusing to think about the uncertainty of her future. And she'd been doing great at self-acceptance, at living each day as it came, right up to the moment when her ex had changed his mind about wanting children of his own, cheated and made Sadie feel worthless for something out of her control.

Although hadn't a part of her always known his grand declarations and big dreams and promises had been too good to be true?

Roman frowned, squeezing her fingers. 'I'm sorry to hear that, Sadie.'

Realising that she'd shared a deeply personal detail with a man she was desperately trying to keep at arm's length, emotionally, she batted away his concern. 'It's fine.'

Because of Roman, because of that night in Vienna, she no longer deserved his empathy. She'd been beyond lucky. She'd been gifted Milly. But as tonight proved, living in the moment worked, because the future was horribly uncertain.

'After that,' she rushed on, trying not to think how she was withholding one key piece of information, 'I was drawn to paediatrics. Like you I sidestepped into it and found a rewarding career that I love.'

'Is that why you're single? The infertility?' he asked, his voice soft, his thumb stroking the palm of her hand in the hypnotic way that loosened Sadie's tongue.

'Kind of,' she said, glad that she could at least be honest about one thing. 'The night I met you was my first Valentine's Day as a single woman in six years.'

He nodded, urging her to continue, his stare reminding her of the way he'd looked at her that night.

'My ex denied that my infertility bothered him for the whole time we were together,' she continued. 'I'd told him about my diagnosis of POI, primary ovarian insufficiency on our first date. I thought I'd come to terms with it, accepted that I would never have children, but I had a career I loved and a great partner. But his promises were lies. He changed his mind, cheated on me and left.'

Her smile felt brittle, but she forced herself to hold Roman's stare. She didn't want his pity. She'd toughened up since then, learned not to take people at face value. If that meant she sometimes expected the worst, that was a small price to pay for her protection.

'I'm sorry you were so badly betrayed.' Roman's eyes turned dark and stormy with repressed emotion. 'He obviously didn't deserve you.'

They stared at each other, their hands still clasped, the fragments of their pain scattered all around them like confetti. She hardly knew this man, but they'd shared so much: passion, secrets, the miraculous creation of a life.

Pressure built in Sadie's chest.

The words *Don't feel too sorry for me because I had your daughter* strained the back of her throat, clamouring to be set free.

Instead she whispered, 'So what now?'

Her fingers were still entwined with his, a reminder of the burning heat of his touch all over her body. A sensible woman would move, but she couldn't seem to make her hand obey.

How was it possible to feel so close to someone she'd known a matter of days? But as she'd learned from her years spent with Mark, time alone was no guarantee of intimacy.

'Now we've laid everything out in the open, I was going to suggest that we be friends,' he admitted, still stroking her palm in a way that was far from friendly while the heat in his stare sent darts of arousal pooling in her pelvis.

Except she *hadn't* told him everything. She was holding back the most important fact.

'But I think we should acknowledge our ongoing chemistry,' he said, staring into her eyes as if she fascinated him, as if he couldn't look away, as if some lonely, broken part of him recognised the same in Sadie, 'which kind of complicates things.'

'It does,' she agreed, the rush of blood to her head dizzying.

His eyes blazed at her admission. 'I can't deny that when I saw you at the hospital I envisaged us getting to know each other better while I'm in London, perhaps going out on a few casual dates, because now you understand why I'm not interested in dating anyone seriously.'

Because he was still grieving, still in love with his wife.

Sadie nodded, her head woolly with guilt and confusion, her heart aching with dashed hope and irrational disappointment. 'I totally understand.'

Except she wished it could be different, for Milly's sake, and perhaps for her own, too.

Then another thought occurred. The auction!

'Listen, I'd be happy to talk to Sammy, to persuade her to find someone else to volunteer to be our eligible doctor. You shouldn't feel coerced or uncomfortable. After all, it's just a silly fundraiser and not important in the grand scheme of things.'

'Look at you, protecting my honour.' He smiled and Sadie's heart skipped a beat.

He shook his head. 'But I said I would do it, and I'm a man of my word. Believe it or not, I allowed myself to be coerced because I was trying to forget about this amazing woman I met in Vienna.'

He'd been thinking about her all this time? Struggled, just like her, to forget about their night together? Dumbfounded, Sadie blinked, ensnared by the desire she saw in his eyes, by the memories of how good they'd been together, physically, by the certainty that they would still rock each other's world.

But now that she knew him better, she felt as if she could tell him anything. Just not about Milly. Not tonight.

'You were a balm to the soul I didn't know I needed that night,' he went on, 'so thank you.' He raised her fingers to his lips and kissed them like an old-fashioned hero.

'You made me feel desirable again that night, so thank you, too.' Sadie all but combusted as the sexy half-smile tugged at his mouth.

Did he too feel this deepening connection that left Sadie bewildered, because, no matter how strong, it could only ever be temporary? It might even be non-existent once she'd told him about Milly.

As if answering her unasked question, his stare dipped to her mouth.

Only the knowledge of Milly waiting at home stopped Sadie from leaning in for a kiss.

'I think I should go,' she said, slipping her hand from the comfort of his as prickles of guilt and confusion made her itchy under her sweater.

Their situation was indeed complicated. She needed to focus on finding the right moment to tell him about his daughter and on preparing herself for his likely reaction. Indulging in their chemistry now would only make things worse.

She reached for her phone and ordered a ride, eager to get away from him to clear her thoughts. She needed to forget about how good it would be to kiss him again so that the next time they met, she'd be ready to break her news.

Roman nodded, a brief flicker of disappointment in his stare.

'Can I walk you home, make sure you're safe?' he asked as they headed for the bar where he paid for their drinks.

Sadie saw that his offer wasn't a line. Roman wasn't that kind of man. But Milly was at home with Grace and prolonging his company meant prolonging the torture of wanting something she couldn't have.

Flustered by the conflicting desires tugging her off balance, she waved her phone. 'I've just ordered a ride, actually, but thanks.'

She needed to be careful. For all their sakes.

She couldn't allow her feelings for him, her attraction and compassion to cloud her judgement.

'Okay. Do you mind if I wait with you?' he asked, holding the door open.

'Of course not.'

As they waited outside, Sadie returned to the one light topic of conversation that felt safe. 'I was thinking… Do you own a tux? It might add an elegance to the auction. Get pulses racing and loosen up the wallets of the bidders a little, although your scrubs would also do the job, just fine.'

The idea of other women drooling over Roman gave her chills she had no right to feel. Just because they'd spent one night as lovers a year ago didn't make him her property.

'I can hire a tux. But you like the surgeon look, huh?' He smiled, knowingly, his eyes full of playful sparkle. 'I think the word you used was *gorgeous.*'

She rolled her eyes, laughing, but it was pointless denying their chemistry. 'Chocolate cake is gorgeous, that doesn't mean it's a good idea to indulge.'

He stepped close, ducked his head and whispered, 'Except once you've indulged, you know how good it will taste next time…'

Sadie shuddered with excitement and longing. He was right. Once wasn't enough.

Before she could make a mistake and kiss him again, a car pulled up at the kerb.

Sadie checked the registration. 'That's my ride.' Relief flooded her system.

Roman cast the driver an assessing once-over, resting his hand on her waist. 'Share your journey with me, so I'll know when you get home safely.'

'I will.' Sadie nodded, touched by his concern and horribly turned on. Now that it was time to part, she didn't want to leave him after the emotional roller coaster of their evening, after everything he'd shared.

'Will you be okay, you know...after our talk?' She hated the idea of him being alone with his grief and his pain, and his memories, when she had their beautiful baby girl to cuddle.

'I will. Goodnight, Sadie.' He swooped down and pressed a swift kiss to her cheek as he'd done when he'd greeted her earlier.

She froze, poised for it to last too long, for it to turn into something heated. She could so easily raise her face to his until their lips connected. His strong arms would encircle her, his hand between her shoulder blades. Their lips would lock with passion while their bodies met once more from mouth to thigh...

It would feel so good. Better, perhaps, than the last time when they'd been total strangers.

But their situation was more complex now. This time there would be no walking away unscathed. She cared about Roman. How could she not? He was Milly's father. A kind and honourable and broken man.

Wary of undoing the fragile emotional ties they'd woven in the bar, she stepped back.

It was only their daughter, waiting at home for her last feed, that gave her the strength to hurry into the waiting car.

Later that night, still horribly conflicted, she hugged a sleeping Milly, who was warm and safe and replete after her feed. The baby's downy hair tickled Sadie's lips as she pressed a kiss to their daughter's forehead.

'I was wrong about your father,' she whispered, thinking about the final text he'd sent shortly after she'd arrived home.

Thanks for letting me know you're safe and thanks for listening.

'He's complex. Hurting. I just hope that when he finally meets you, you bring him as much joy as you've brought me.'

Her final thought just before she fell asleep was that she was in an impossible position. She couldn't fall back into bed with him, no matter how much she wanted to. But until she found the perfect moment, she couldn't tell him the news she hoped would be welcome. She had no idea what to do next, but she'd have to do it soon, before her options became even more limited.

CHAPTER SIX

TWO DAYS LATER, in the early hours of the morning, Sadie sat at the bedside of eight-year-old Josh, her stare obsessively drawn to the monitor recording his oxygen saturation levels, pulse and respiratory rate. The young boy, who was also one of Roman's patients, had been admitted a week ago for an urgent splenectomy following injuries sustained in a car crash. He'd lost a lot of blood, requiring a transfusion, and had spent several days post-op on ICU.

He'd already been through so much, and today, at the start of Sadie's night shift, Josh had spiked a fever. Sadie had diagnosed his latest setback—a post-op chest infection that required close monitoring.

She shifted in the hard plastic chair, looking down at the sleeping boy. The unease making her extra watchful tonight was all tangled up with her constant thoughts of Roman, who'd lost a son around this boy's age. Ever since he'd bravely shared his story with her, she hadn't been able to get Roman off her mind.

Roman's team had been on call, the ward busy as usual, so they'd only seen each other from a distance a few times, shared a nod of greeting and a secret look. Sadie had even texted him 'Thinking of you' messages.

But as the days passed, the urge to track him down and blurt out her secret grew stronger.

Before she could wonder for the millionth time just how she would utter the words *You have a daughter*, the curtains around Josh's bed swished aside and Roman appeared, as if he'd heard his name whisper through her mind.

His brief smile for Sadie lit her up inside.

'How is he doing?' he asked, glancing at the monitors, his concern for their patient mirroring her own.

She rose and joined him at the foot of the bed, close but not touching, the air between them charged with electricity.

'He's stable at the moment,' she said in a hushed voice, some of the tension leaving her now that Roman was here to share Josh's care. 'I've started broad spectrum IV antibiotics and made an urgent referral for physiotherapy for the morning. Hopefully we can get on top of the infection.'

The last thing anyone wanted was to see Josh back in ICU.

'Let's talk in the office,' Roman said, touching her arm and leading the way just as Josh's nurse arrived to repeat his observations and note them on his bedside chart.

'I encouraged his parents to grab a hot drink and some toast in the family room,' Sadie said as they entered the small ward office. She'd left Josh's chest film displayed on the monitor, and Roman paused to examine the X-ray.

'The consolidation is subtle; good spotting,' Roman said, flicking her an impressed smile that, despite her concern for this patient, did silly things to her already elevated pulse.

Sadie nodded, unable to shake her unease, probably because, she couldn't help but draw parallels between Josh and Roman's son.

Looking at him now, knowing that Milly shared his blue eyes, she wondered what Roman's boy had been like. Had he looked like his father? Would baby Milly remind Roman of her half-brother? And how could he possibly feel joy for his daughter, having lost his son in such a sudden and senseless way?

'You're worried,' he stated, his stare full of understanding and compassion, because they shared a profession that often took an emotional toll.

The stakes seemed higher in paediatrics than

adult medicine. Some young patients faced more hurdles than others for no rhyme or reason. Being objective was a big part of their job.

'A little,' she admitted with a small sigh. 'We managed to get a sputum sample for the lab before we started the antibiotics.'

Maybe because she was now a mother, or maybe because she knew what Roman had been through, Sadie couldn't help but see every case through the eyes of a parent.

'Hopefully we'll be able to target the correct pathogen with our treatment.' Sadie shrugged, looking away from Roman's probing stare because she could read him so easily now that she understood his past.

Could he read her in the same way? Could he see that, in addition to her patients, Sadie was worried for them: her, Milly and Roman?

'Then you're doing everything you can,' he said, stepping closer to rest a hand on her shoulder. 'Tell me what else is bothering you.'

Of course he would intuitively sense Sadie's hesitation in Josh's case. He was a good doctor, and he had personal experience of how suddenly things could go wrong.

'I don't know.' Sadie glanced at her feet because she was hiding something life-changing from him.

Admitting that she was worried for this patient

felt like admitting that she was worried for the future she tried to avoid examining.

'Sometimes it's hard to stay detached…' she said.

From work… From him… From wanting impossible things…

She'd perfected living in the moment, but, in light of Roman's tragic past, she couldn't help but wonder if they'd be able to find a way to make their complex and emotionally charged situation work. She didn't want any of them to be hurt, but of course she couldn't voice any of that.

'Sometimes a patient just gets to you.' Roman tilted his head, understanding in his eyes. 'We're only human.'

That he understood her professional concerns so well left her irrationally close to tears.

'Things always feel more serious in the middle of the night.' He slid his hand down the length of her arm and took her hand. 'I'll check in with you both again when the sun's up. Fresh perspective.'

Sadie nodded, grateful for his support, basking in the heat of his illicit touch that she'd grown to expect in just these few short days. Desperation to unburden herself fully rose up in her chest. But the more time that passed, the harder it was to find the right moment to tell him about their baby.

It was three a.m. Roman would be on his way back to Theatre. He needed to work. She couldn't be selfish, just because her secret weighed more and more heavily.

'How are *you* doing since we talked the other night?' She clung to his hand. 'I haven't been able to stop thinking about you. Worrying. Our work must be triggering sometimes.'

She'd watched him on the ward these past few days, her respect for him growing, alongside her desire. His calm manner never failed to put both patients and parents at ease, just as he'd reassured Sadie tonight. He always seemed to be the last surgeon to go home and the first one there in the morning. Even now, he'd obviously come up to the ward in between surgeries to check on the sickest of his patients.

Seriously attractive dedication.

'You don't have to worry about me.' He smiled a heartbreaking little half-smile, squeezing her fingers so a thrill zapped up her arm. 'I've developed coping strategies over the years, some of which probably aren't too healthy—you might have noticed I'm a bit of a workaholic.'

Sadie's heart fought its way into her throat as they stared at each other. If only they were anywhere but at work. She would hold him, be there for him the way he was there for her tonight, show him that he wasn't alone.

Except he chose to be alone. That was how he coped.

Her stomach fell, her feelings redundant.

As if deciding he could trust her with his most honest response, Roman sobered. 'Besides, I'm more scared to forget than to remember.'

The huge lump in her throat made breathing hard. 'Scared to forget your family?'

Her voice was an awed whisper that he trusted her with such a deeply private admission. But it also brough fresh waves of guilt that she was carrying such a monumental secret.

Roman gave a curt nod, his eyes tortured. 'My son in particular. I had many more years of memories with Karolina.'

'I'm sorry.' She gripped his hand tighter, aware that she should let them both go back to work. 'Do you mind me asking—what was your son's name?'

'I don't mind. His name was Mikolas.' His eyes shone with love for his little boy. 'We called him Miko.'

'Miko.' Sadie said, blinking away the burn of tears. 'I like that.'

The name painted a picture of an energetic little boy, with a contagious giggle and Roman's cheeky smile. Surely a man with Roman's capacity for love and commitment would, in time, welcome Milly into his heart?

They stood in silence, sad smiles fading. The tension in the room shifted.

'You have a big heart, Sadie.' He cupped her cheek and swiped his thumb over her cheekbone, his touch a brand, sharpening her awareness of every inch of him.

Sadie's stare latched onto the intricate depths of his irises. 'So do you,' she whispered.

'Basic job requirement.' He shrugged, the light-hearted comment most likely offered as a lifeline, an escape from the moment of intimacy into which they'd somehow stumbled.

But Sadie was right where she wanted to be.

'It makes you a good doctor,' he continued, his stare moving over her face, 'one who relates easily to people. But also makes you vulnerable to compassion fatigue. Look after yourself, okay?'

Sadie nodded, overwhelmed that he cared. She *was* tired, but her fatigue came from fighting this chemistry every time they spoke. She was tired of second-guessing her feelings. Sometimes, you had to follow your instincts, even when they'd been brought into question by your past mistakes.

Vienna hadn't been a mistake.

Surely one more kiss wouldn't be either.

She closed the gap, her heartbeat pulsing in her fingertips, clanging in her ears, like a roar.

Roman's expression shifted from conflicted to surrender.

He gripped her face in both hands, their lips connecting.

Desperation clawed at Sadie. Hot. Urgent. Crazed.

She tugged his neck and parted her lips, matching the passion of his kiss. Zero hesitation.

It *was* as good as before. Better.

Sadie closed her eyes as his arms gripped her so tightly, she couldn't breathe. But she didn't want to breathe in case she came to her senses. In case Roman came to his.

They were kissing. At work.

Outside the room, the ward was quiet, most of the patients asleep while the night staff made silent rounds. But they'd left the door ajar. Anyone could walk in. Not that Sadie could bring herself to stop.

Roman slid his hands around her waist. She gripped his bunched shoulders, tunnelled her fingers into his hair as she inched them towards the desk, resting her butt on the edge. She tangled her tongue with his, needing to condense everything she wanted, everything she needed into this moment of madness.

Soon she'd stop. Any second now.

Roman grunted, pressing his body between her parted thighs, snatching kiss after kiss in a frantic rush that told Sadie he'd struggled with wanting her every inch as much as she'd fought her desire for him.

Gifting herself one last minute of bliss, Sadie kissed him back, finally admitting that, for her, this had been inevitable from the moment he'd walked onto her ward. It didn't matter that it could only be temporary. Sadie was an expert at living in the moment.

Except there was one thing that *did* matter: Milly. Roman's daughter, the baby they'd made the last time they'd allowed their passion to override all else. A baby he knew nothing about.

With a sickening lurch of her stomach, she tore her mouth away.

'We can't do this.' She panted, guilt a scald creeping over her skin.

It took monumental effort to shove at his shoulders, but she succeeded, standing and moving away.

'Of course,' he said, his expression dazed and confused and then contrite.

He glanced at the door behind him and scrubbed a hand over his face. 'I'm sorry. I wasn't thinking.'

Sadie shook her head violently. If only their problems were simply an ill-judged smooch in the workplace. But they had bigger issues, and, perfect timing or not, Sadie could delay no longer, her secret pressing down on her like a lead straightjacket.

She gripped his arm, willing him to show the same caring and compassionate side that emerged for his patients and colleagues. The time had come to tell him. Even if it ruined the connection they shared. Even if her news was devastating. Even if he reacted with anger and accusation and wanted nothing to do with darling Milly, it was time Roman knew about his daughter.

Breathing hard, Roman's head spun like a case of vertigo after being so violently ripped back to his senses.

'No, I'm sorry.' Sadie gripped his arm, shook her head again, a deep frown creasing her brow and tugging down her kiss-swollen lips.

She was so beautiful. That she'd leaned on him for reassurance tonight, confided her clinical concerns for their patient, shown concern for Roman and even asked about Miko had finally pushed him to breaking point.

He wanted her.

He knew it was wrong to indulge at work, but he'd also recalled how right it had felt to kiss her the first time.

'Roman, we need to talk.' Her hand fell away, the new resolve in her tone the bucket of cold water to the face he needed.

He nodded, grappling with his breathlessness. 'That was really unprofessional of me, Sadie. I shouldn't have touched you. I'm sorry.'

What had he been thinking kissing a junior colleague at work? But from the moment she'd smiled at his son's name, he'd known he couldn't fight their chemistry any longer.

Even now, with shame nipping at his heels, he wanted her still.

'No.' She frowned, staring with what looked like fear in her eyes. 'I wanted to kiss you. It's not that, it's just—' She broke off, nervously licking the soft lips that had a second ago melded to his with the passion he remembered. 'I need to tell you something.'

When she looked up the determination on her face made his heated blood run cold.

'Okay.' Trying to get his heart rate under control, Roman stepped back, away from the temptation of Sadie. 'What is it?'

Reminding him of that first confusing day when they'd talked in this very office, Sadie paced to the desk and then faced him once more.

'I should have told you before.' She wrung her hands. 'I planned to tell you. I almost did. So many times. I just…couldn't seem to find the right moment.'

She twisted her mouth as if in anguish. 'And

I know now isn't ideal…because it's the middle of the night and we both have work to do…but I have to tell you, because we kissed and—'

This time he struggled to find her nervous rambling cute. 'What's wrong? Tell me now,' he ordered, his mind going to dark places. 'Please, Sadie.'

Trepidation was a tight fist around his heart. Memories slayed him; that terrible night four years ago when he'd stood in a dark hospital corridor while some poor young emergency doctor had given him the news no person ever wanted to hear.

'Please don't be angry.' Sadie swallowed, her stare imploring. 'I didn't want to hurt you…'

Hurt him? What had she done?

'Just tell me what's wrong.' Roman's pulse leaped, pumping trickles of adrenaline around his blood. His imagination was running wild. 'Are you ill? About to emigrate? Have you met someone else?'

Sadie shook her head. 'Nothing's wrong. Everything is fine. It's just—' She looked down at her hands and Roman wanted to tear at his hair in frustration.

The seconds pulsed through him like electric shocks. He had to draw on every scrap of patience he possessed to wait for her to say the upsetting words she was holding back.

Finally, her shoulders sagged, her eyes locked to his. 'I had a baby,' she said, expelling the announcement on a rush of air.

Roman took a few seconds to catch up, ninety per cent of his brain still stuck on how fantastic it had been to have her back in his arms and the other ten per cent braced for her announcement of bad news.

'Oh… That's wonderful. Amazing. Congratulations.' He took her hands, overjoyed that the fertility issues she'd confessed to him had been overcome. 'But that's happy news, isn't it?'

She didn't look happy. She looked nauseated as she offered a feeble nod. 'It's wonderful.'

Relief pooled in his veins. She wasn't sick, just a mother.

'So are you seeing someone?' He winced, thinking about their incendiary kiss, about how he might have been utterly carried away if they hadn't been at work. 'You should have told me. I would never have kissed you if I'd known.'

Now that the shock had worn off, hollowness rushed in. She *was* seeing someone. He had no right to kiss her, no prior claim. She deserved to be happy, deserved so much more than Roman had to give.

'I'm not seeing anyone,' she said flatly, desperation in her eyes. 'You don't understand…'

'Then explain it to me.' He was trying to follow, but she wasn't making much sense. She was doing that evasive thing again…

'I haven't slept with anyone since you. Since Vienna.'

Roman frowned, the lust fog in his brain finally clearing as if he'd just broken the surface of the water after a deep-sea dive.

His stunned gasp sounded in his head.

Sadie had given birth to *his* baby.

Sadie nodded, seeing that his understanding had finally dawned. 'We um…made a baby last Valentine's.'

A baby…? Roman's first thought turned his blood to ice. 'Did something happen? To the baby?'

It must have been the worst thing imaginable. Why else would she keep this a secret from him all this time?

Sadie frowned, gripping his hands tight so his focus sharpened on her mouth. 'Nothing happened. Nothing's wrong. She's beautiful. A healthy two-month-old.'

'What…?' The floor tilted under Roman's feet. He reached out to steady himself on the edge of the desk. This couldn't be happening.

He had a baby. Another child. A two-month old.

'We used protection,' he muttered, blindly

scrambling for the first idiotic thought to enter his head. But he was deliberately careful. He'd never wanted to be a father again.

'You said you couldn't have children.' If he'd been able to think, he might not have chosen such accusatory statements, but he had no thoughts that made sense. This must be some sort of joke.

Sadie nodded, her sympathetic stare and her hand clutching his all the confirmation he required that her words were true. 'I know. She's a tiny little miracle. Her name is Milly.'

Milly… He swallowed, his throat full of sawdust.

Stunned, Roman shook his head. 'No… I can't… No…'

A baby…? A miracle baby. A baby he knew nothing about.

'Why didn't you tell me sooner?' Staring at Sadie, he tried to deflect the emotions pounding him like blows from a heavyweight boxer.

He welcomed the pain; he'd lived with it so long. Fresh guilt sliced through him, like slashes from a scalpel. Miko was his baby. He loved Miko.

'I'm sorry,' Sadie said, her eyes brimming with tears. 'I know it's a shock for you. I wanted to break the news better than this.'

Nausea gripped him, disbelief rendering him speechless.

He closed his eyes, but that didn't help, because all he could see was his beloved son as a two-month-old. How could he possibly be a father again when he was so…broken? How could he be what a child needed when he'd spent so long alone, shutting down his need for other people? How would he love another child when his heart was full with Karolina and Miko?

'If I'd had any way of contacting you during the past eleven months,' Sadie continued with her explanation, 'I would have told you as soon as I found out I was pregnant. And when you showed up here, I was so shocked that I couldn't find the words. I never intended to keep it from you. I planned to tell you that first day. But then I was still attracted to you and I'd just found out that you were our eligible doctor and the moment passed. After that, I just couldn't seem to find the right time.'

He opened his eyes. The fear lacing his blood was as fresh as the moment he'd received a bad-news call from the hospital four years ago.

'Is she okay?' he gritted out, some innate protective instinct in him needing confirmation, even though he didn't know this child. His child.

'She's fine. Perfect,' Sadie rushed to reassure him as her tears spilled over, landing on her cheeks. 'I'm so sorry you had to find out this way.'

'So am I...' Still dazed by the mind-bending news, Roman looked away. He was in survival mode, his empathy for Sadie's anguish missing in action while he tried to process the news he'd never thought he'd experience again.

'I called the hotel in Vienna, when I was pregnant,' Sadie added. 'But even if I'd known your name, they have a policy to protect guests' privacy.'

She glanced down at her twisting hands. 'I planned to tell you that night at the bar, but then you shared your past with me and I was scared that my news would upset you even more.'

Just then, his pager emitted its silence-shattering tone. Roman scrubbed his hand through his hair and cancelled it, mumbling, 'I need to go back to Theatre.'

'Of course.' Sadie collected herself, swiping the tears from her cheeks. Perhaps sensing how overwhelmed he felt, she reached for his hand. 'Roman, don't worry; I don't expect anything from you. I know you're leaving London soon. I know you didn't want another child.'

She meant what he'd said in Vienna about marriage and kids. What he'd reiterated on several occasions since seeing her again. Of course he hadn't wanted another child. He never again wanted to experience the pain of loving and losing.

Only Sadie's miracle had intervened. His daughter was here anyway.

Numb, he stared at her hand on his, shattered anew by Sadie's blotchy face and haunted eyes. Her confession had taken its toll on them both.

She dropped his hand. 'I know how you feel about it and it's okay,' she whispered.

'Do you know how I feel?' he said, shaking his head.

A child changed everything. Right now, he didn't even know which way was up. 'Because I can't even begin to verbalise my feelings.'

She nodded, a frown of concern on her face as she watched him inch towards the door. 'That's fine, too.'

Her teeth snagged her bottom lip, catching Roman's gaze.

It seemed like hours since they'd kissed. Another lifetime.

If only the constant pull of their chemistry were his most pressing consideration. Now there were bigger issues to contemplate. Now Sadie and he weren't simply past lovers, reunited, they were parents. Now there was a tiny baby called Milly.

Overwhelmed by his conflicting emotions, he rushed back to Theatre, choked by fear and grief.

Was he capable of being a father again? Could he love another child? Would a new baby diminish his precious memories of Miko even further? And could he bear to find out?

CHAPTER SEVEN

Two DAYS LATER, a distracted Sadie headed to the paediatric multidisciplinary meeting, or MDM: a once-weekly team discussion where professionals from different specialities reviewed patients' diagnoses, care and treatment options.

As she sneaked quietly into the room where the MDM was already under way her heart raced at the possibility that Roman might be there. She hadn't seen him since that fateful night they'd kissed and she'd told him about Milly. Guilt for the way it had eventually unfolded had stopped her from reaching out to him; he obviously needed space to think.

The room was in darkness while a radiologist explained the MRI scan findings displayed on a large projector screen. Sadie took a seat near the back and scanned the occupied seats for a glimpse of Roman.

He sat in the front row, next to the two paediatric oncologists, his handsome profile highlighted by the glow from the screen. Her heart rate accelerated with longing; they'd been growing so close. Now everything was uncertain.

Sadie sat still, trying not to draw attention to herself.

Part of her had been relieved by his absence on the ward these past two days. If he'd appeared while Sadie was there, she might have had to face his understandable hurt that she'd kept her news a secret, or, worse, witness again his pain and confusion. It had been hard enough to watch the first time around, when all that lovely desire following their kiss had been slashed and shredded by guilt.

Who could blame him for his hesitance to embrace Milly? Sadie had given him a lot to process and he was still grieving for his family. But the impatience to know where she and Milly stood, one way or another, was a constant itch under her skin.

In allowing him space to work through the knowledge that he was once more a father, Sadie had essentially been shut out, forced to ponder the future and fill in the blanks, to contemplate the dreaded *what ifs*.

What if, because of his past loss, he was incapable of loving Milly? What if he was too broken to even welcome their baby into his life? What if, when he left London, she never saw him again and their darling and innocent daughter grew up never knowing her intelligent and caring father?

While she would understand his reasons, his rejection of their precious daughter would still be devastating.

Sadie had never considered herself a coward, but right now, she wasn't certain which was worse: knowing those answers or her current state of ignorance.

Sick to her stomach with fear and longing, Sadie startled as the room lights came on while, around her, the case discussion continued.

'So we're looking at a stage two nephroblastoma,' Roman said, his deep and confident voice jangling Sadie's nerves. 'Would you want to give neoadjuvant chemo in this case?' he asked the medical oncologist at his side. 'Or is everyone happy for me to go in and operate?'

How could he sound so…normal, when Sadie felt as though she'd been sleep-walking through her life?

With his question hanging in the air, he cast his eyes around the room for corroboration from the assembled team.

His stare landed on Sadie.

She froze, her breath catching in her throat as their eyes locked for a split second before he turned away to resume the discussion.

Sadie swallowed, her mouth dry. How could she still want him so violently when they had monumental issues to discuss and try to overcome? How could she crave his touch, his kiss, the way he'd opened up to her emotionally, when he'd so obviously withdrawn to lick his wounds?

Fear was her constant companion. Fear that she'd hurt Roman, irreparably. That she'd ruined any chance of them being a parenting team. That he'd want nothing to do with her, or beloved Milly.

With a treatment plan in place for Roman's nephroblastoma patient, the discussion continued to other cases on the list. Sadie tried her best to focus on the clinical deliberation taking place, but her gaze returned to the back of Roman's head, time and again, as if willing him to be okay, willing him to let her back in.

As the meeting wrapped up, Sadie stood and made a beeline for the exit, her stomach on the floor with defeat. How could she have forgotten her own resolve to live for the moment? She and Milly were fine as they were. They'd be fine whatever Roman decided. Milly's happiness and stability were all that truly mattered.

'Dr Barnes, a word, please.' Roman's voice halted her in her tracks.

Sadie paused, ducking into in a doorway to

avoid the flow of foot traffic leaving the MDM, her nerves now completely shredded.

Today, Roman was wearing a navy-blue suit, as if deliberately taunting her with his out-of-reach hotness. Her stare caressed the crisp tailoring moulded to his broad shoulders and trim waist. The shirt and tie gave him a sophisticated look that almost buckled Sadie's knees. It wasn't fair that he looked so good.

Swallowing the lump of lust and trepidation in her throat, she searched his stare for some clue of how he was feeling on the inside, spying fatigue around his eyes.

'Thanks for waiting,' he said, his body stiff with formality, as if they were complete strangers. 'How are you?'

He slung his hands in his trouser pockets and Sadie withered a little, desperate for his touch, desperate to know things between them would be okay, desperate for the emotional closeness they'd shared when he'd been comfortable enough in her to confide his deepest pain.

She genuinely cared that he might be suffering.

'I'm fine, Dr Ježek. How are you?' Sadie stepped deeper into the alcove, aware that the MDM room was still emptying of their colleagues, not the optimal venue for a private conversation.

How could they act so...distant when they'd

made a Valentine's Day baby together? The last time they'd worked together, they'd all but ripped off each other's clothes and had sex on the desk. No matter what else was going on between them, for Sadie, the attraction was as strong as ever.

Except she had no idea how he was feeling.

Glancing over his shoulder to ensure they were alone, Roman stepped closer. Catching her totally unawares, he reached for her hand. 'Listen, I wanted to apologise.'

His voice was low, husky with emotion.

'Please, you haven't done anything wrong. There's no need to apologise.' Excited and confused by his touch, Sadie used all her strength to slip her hand from his.

There was no point indulging her attraction when their connection was now so fragile. Emotionally, things between them seemed to have gone a few steps backwards. Now that he was close, she saw the turmoil in his eyes, the dark smudges beneath as if he hadn't been sleeping.

Her news had clearly left him tormented.

The lump returned to her throat, her heart aching for this honourable but wounded man, her spirit crushed for darling, innocent Milly.

'There is,' he said, his stare stony as if he was holding his emotions in check. 'Last time we spoke I was...overwhelmed. I reacted badly.'

He held her stare, his hand reaching for hers

again before he thought better of it and dropped his arm to his side. 'I came across as accusing, and that wasn't my intention.'

'I understood. It was a shock for you.' Compassion rose up in Sadie like a surging wave. Of course he'd be overwhelmed. She'd had nine months to come to terms with the fact that they'd made a baby.

She couldn't be angry with him; it might be easier if she could.

'I feel horribly guilty about that night, if it's any consolation. Kissing you at work,' she whispered, 'and then dropping that bombshell…'

She should have found a way to tell him sooner, somewhere private.

His stare softened, the ghost of his playful smile tugging his lips. 'There's no need to feel guilty.' A shrug, a sparkle in his eyes. 'And I too must hold my hand up and take responsibility for the kiss.' He glanced at her mouth, sending sparks along her nerves. 'Not my finest decision, so, again, I apologise.'

Flames engulfed Sadie's body, even as she agonised over his meaning. Did he regret kissing her? Or just regret kissing her at work? But what did it matter when they had bigger issues to resolve, when he seemed a million miles away?

Peering over his shoulder, confirming that they were still alone, Sadie braved another question.

'I don't want to rush you—I've been giving you breathing space—but have you had any thoughts on what you want to do?'

She held her breath, watched doubt flit over his expression, her stomach swooping with disappointment. She could absolutely raise Milly alone. But she wanted Milly and Roman to have a relationship, as long as it was a mutually positive thing.

He sighed, glancing up at the ceiling, as if the weight of the world rested on his shoulders, telling Sadie everything she needed to know.

'I've had too many thoughts to count.' He faced her, his stare sincere. 'This news has brought up a lot of feelings I thought I'd already dealt with. I'm questioning everything. I wish I could give you answers, but you might need to give me a little more time. Is that okay?'

Sadie swallowed, crushed anew for unsuspecting Milly and heartsore for broken Roman. 'Of course. I respect your honesty and I understand.'

It was true. He'd been through so much loss. Given his circumstances, it would be hard for Sadie to trust less considered or profuse reactions. If he couldn't commit to knowing his daughter, it might be better for them never to meet.

'I'm grateful, actually,' she said, 'that you

aren't rushing to make promises that you might not be ready to keep.'

Except she couldn't help the tiny flicker of hope that one day he would embrace their beautiful daughter into his life.

Sensing her disappointment, he reached for her hand once more, his gaze pleading, tearing her heart to shreds. 'I wish it were just simple joy that I was feeling. Ordinarily, that's what your news would deserve. It's what I long to feel.'

Sadie nodded, too choked to speak, too comforted by his touch. She wished she could throw her arms around him.

'But I'm all over the place, Sadie. My grief has resurfaced. I don't know which way is up. And until I've worked through some of these feelings, it wouldn't be fair to you or to Milly to rush into anything.'

Sadie blinked up at him, her eyes smarting as she dragged in a deep breath for courage. He was so wonderful, so different from her ex. 'You're right, and I appreciate that, believe me.'

Roman's cautious but honest response was way better than the kind of grand declaration Mark would have made but then failed to deliver upon. This way, Sadie was no worse off for having told Roman about Milly, her and the baby's day-to-day routine unchanged.

Except waiting, seeing him at work, wanting him despite it all, was its own brand of torture.

'Where is she now?' he asked on a whisper, his stare stormy with repressed emotions. 'What happens to Milly while you're at work?'

Even while he processed the life-changing news while also dealing with renewed grief, he was thinking about the daughter they'd made.

Her heart lurched, reaching for him. 'She's at home, with my sister. Grace is a trained nanny. There's no one I trust more.'

She wanted him to know that his daughter was safe and cared for, even if he wasn't, and might never be, ready to be her father.

He nodded, appeased, but his jaw clenched as if he was holding back further questions.

'Would you like to see a picture of her?' Sadie asked, emboldened by the fact that he clearly cared, but braced for his answer. 'It's okay if you want to say no.'

She didn't want to rush him, but he was hurting, not indifferent.

How awful that, for Roman, Sadie's miracle gift, her precious adored baby, brought such heart-rending conflict of emotion. On the one hand, he was understandably curious and on the other, overwhelmed by grief and doubt.

He nodded, visibly swallowing as if he couldn't trust himself to speak.

Her stomach twisting with apprehension, Sadie took her phone from her pocket and brought up a recent baby photo: Milly asleep like an angel, her tiny fingers curled into a chubby fist.

Roman took the device, his hand trembling and his stare haunted.

She'd never seen him uncertain of anything.

His eyes scoured the image, one hand covering his mouth as if to hold in a primal sound. Of anguish or joy or both, Sadie couldn't tell.

'You can't see from that photo,' she said, her own voice scratchy with empathy and grief for her dreams for Milly, 'but she has your eyes. As soon as she was born, she looked up at me and I recognised them.'

'Just like Miko,' he whispered, his tortured stare glued to the phone.

Sadie's pulse pounded in her temples, hope blooming; surely his reaction to the sight of his daughter was promising?

Just then, Sadie's phone rang, its piercing trill breaking the moment of strange and stilted intimacy.

Roman handed the device back and scrubbed a hand over his haggard face.

Sadie spoke to the nurse from Sunshine Ward, glancing Roman's way with concern when she heard the news.

'It's Josh,' she said, work temporarily resetting her priorities. 'He's gone off. Saturations dropping. Tachypnoea. Cyanosis. I need to go.'

Milly and Roman's relationship would have to wait.

'I'll come with you.'

They started running, side by side, making it to the ward within minutes. When they arrived at his bedside, Josh was breathing rapidly, his lips blue despite the oxygen mask covering his nose and mouth.

Sadie placed her stethoscope in her ears and listened to the boy's chest while Roman checked the latest chest X-ray and blood test results and spoke to Josh's nurse.

'Reduced breath sounds on the right,' Sadie informed Roman, who placed his hand on the boy's chest, before listening for breath sounds with his own stethoscope.

'He has subcutaneous emphysema,' he said, inviting Sadie to palpate Josh's chest, their eyes meeting in the kind of silent communication that had become second nature.

Pneumothorax was a complication of pneumonia, and in Josh's case it seemed that the air was leaking, not only into his chest cavity, causing a partial collapse of the lung, but it was also leaking into the skin and subcutaneous tissues over his ribs.

Was Roman, like her, thinking about Miko?

But for a cruel twist of fate, Roman's son could have ended up in Josh's position, surviving the car crash, hospitalised with complications. But, of course, Roman's son was likely never far from his thoughts. He was probably acutely aware of the parallels.

'Let's wheel Josh into the treatment room,' Roman said, telling Sadie that he intended to stick around and help out. 'We need a portable chest X-ray asap, please,' he added to Sammy, who'd appeared to assess the commotion.

The treatment for pneumothorax was a chest drain. Sadie had done the urgent procedure many times. While Josh's parents were called for their verbal consent, the radiographer arrived to take the chest X-ray that would confirm their diagnosis.

Working with their hunch, Roman and Sadie prepared the equipment they'd need in order to insert a chest drain to alleviate Josh's symptoms.

'You insert the drain, I'll assist,' Roman said, his concern for their patient evident.

'Thank you,' Sadie said, grateful for his ongoing professional support. They stared at each other for a second, as if aware of the other's thoughts.

They might not have the future all figured out—that was how Sadie preferred it—but when it came to their work, they could set their personal issues aside. At the hospital, they had the one thing that mattered: trust.

Roman flashed her a sad but reassuring smile and handed her some gloves.

The digital X-ray confirmed their diagnosis of pneumothorax. While Roman administered a light intravenous sedative to keep Josh calm through the minimally invasive procedure, Sadie swabbed Josh's skin and injected local anaesthetic between his ribs.

Sadie glanced at Roman for the all-clear to proceed.

'Slow and steady,' he said, giving her a nod of encouragement that she lapped up. He was senior, a surgeon. He could have easily commandeered the situation and taken over the procedure or walked off the ward and left her to it. But by staying to assist, he'd shown Sadie that he trusted her to care for their patient.

She couldn't ask for more.

With the procedure complete, the chest drain sited to suck escaped air from the chest cavity so the lung could reinflate, Roman and Sadie left a sleepy Josh to the care of his nurse and his parents.

'You did well,' Roman said as they washed their hands before heading to the ward office where Sadie would type up the incident in Josh's hospital notes.

'Thanks for your help—I've never done it with a surgeon before.' Realising what she'd said, she covered her face in her hands. 'Sorry. That came out wrong.'

But her faux pas had broken the earlier tension.

Roman grinned, the playful flare of heat lingering in his eyes. 'Don't worry, I know what you meant.'

And just like that, many of the doubts that had plagued her these past few days evaporated. At the hospital, they made a good team. Surely with patience and caution and the honesty they'd always shared, they'd get through this. Yes, he needed time to come to terms with the news of Milly's existence, but maybe he also needed... encouragement.

Closing the office door, she stepped close, resting her hand on his arm. They couldn't seem to stop touching each other.

'I've been thinking,' she said, 'and there's absolutely no pressure either way, because I meant what I said about giving you space, but...would you like to meet her? Milly, I mean?'

Tension tugged at the corners of his mouth.

'My sister brings her to the café across the road most lunchtimes,' Sadie rushed on, 'so I can feed her while I grab a sandwich. You'd be very welcome to join us. But if you think it's too soon or a bad idea, that's okay. I just thought...you know...

with us being here and her being right across the street... Actually, I don't know what I thought. You're right; it's overwhelming...'

Catching her off guard, Roman rested the tip of his index finger on her top lip, silencing her. 'Please, no more nervous chatter.'

His hesitant smile turned indulgent in that way that told her he found her amusing. 'I get the idea of what you're saying.'

The burn of his finger against her lips turned her insides to jelly.

'What time will you be there?' he asked non-committally, his hand falling to his side, so Sadie missed his touch all over again.

'One p.m., emergencies notwithstanding of course.'

'I won't make any promises,' he said, reaching for the door handle at his back.

'Okay,' Sadie whispered, both grateful that he wouldn't let her down and disappointed that Milly might go another day without meeting her kind and compassionate father.

Before he left the room, he cast her one final glance, laced with confusion, haunted by pain.

Sadie exhaled her held breath, her hand resting over her pounding heart. His concession was a small step in the right direction, one with which she could live. Now she just needed to set aside the way he made her feel every time they touched, which, despite everything else going on, seemed to be something of an addiction.

CHAPTER EIGHT

ROMAN GLANCED THROUGH the café window, his throat constricted with fear. The place was busy with lunchtime diners, but, attuned to Sadie as he was, he spotted her easily at a table near the back, sitting with a woman who was obviously her identical twin, a buggy between them, facing away so there was no sign of Milly.

He watched Sadie chat to her sister for a few minutes, her stare falling to her phone often. She was clearly waiting for him, apprehensive that he might change his mind about meeting his daughter.

Compassion for Sadie surged through his chest. This situation wasn't easy for either of them. Not only had she felt forced to keep her secret, when their baby must have brought her so much joy, given her fertility issues, but she was also giving him time, because she knew about his past and understood how he must be feeling…torn.

Entranced and curious, fearful and desolate all at once.

Drawn to meet his daughter, as he'd been almost from the first instant he'd known of her existence, Roman entered the café. The minute Sadie had put the idea of today's introduction in his head, he'd struggled to think about anything else. Meeting Milly would of course jeopardise the emotional status quo he'd inhabited since he'd lost Karolina and Miko. But it was too late.

He couldn't pretend that his baby didn't exist, and he could no longer stay away. He needed to see her, just once. Then he could make sense of his conflicted thoughts, make a plan, move forward from the numb void he'd inhabited these past few days.

Roman ordered tea he likely wouldn't be able to drink and headed for Sadie's table.

The two women looked up.

'Grace, this is Roman Ježek,' Sadie said, her voice wary but her eyes alight with a spark of excitement he'd come to depend upon whenever their eyes met. 'Grace is my sister, obviously. The one I told you about,' she added for Roman.

'Hello,' Roman said, smiling at the woman, so much like Sadie, who cared for their daughter while her parents worked.

'Nice to meet you.' Grace stood, nudging the buggy in Sadie's direction and reaching for her bag. 'I'll leave you two alone. I…um…need to make a phone call.'

Grace discreetly melted away.

Roman stared at the hood of the buggy, the feeling that he'd forgotten to do something vital clawing at his insides. Pressure built in his head. He'd imagined this moment a million times since Sadie had informed him of his daughter's existence, but now that it was here, now that he was about to see his baby in the flesh, he feared his legs would buckle.

'Why don't you sit down?' Sadie suggested, attuned somehow to his inner turmoil.

Roman folded himself robotically into the chair, feeling brittle, as one false move would shatter him into a million mismatched shards.

Sadie reached across the table and took his hand. He clung tight.

'Do you want to see her?' Sadie asked, her smile soft with sympathy and understanding.

'Yes,' he said, a catch to his voice that threatened to reveal the cascade of conflicted emotions pouring through him.

Fear because he'd spent the past four long years shoring up his emotions to protect himself from further pain, and might not be able to open himself up once more. Longing to see his child so intense, he had to curl his hands into fists to stop himself from whirling the buggy around. And guilt. Not only because, as broken as he was, he couldn't be the kind of father that his baby deserved, but also because welcoming a new baby into his heart felt like a betrayal of Miko, somehow.

As if in knowing his daughter, he might forget his son.

'She fell asleep after I fed her,' Sadie explained as she wheeled the buggy to face him so the baby came into view.

Time stopped.

She slept with her fists curled beside her face, her delicate eyelashes crescents on her cherubic cheeks.

Ever since Sadie had told him about Milly, Roman had been terrified to make another human connection, one he knew from tragic experience would have the power to tear him apart emotionally. Except fate had other ideas, taking out of his hands his decision to never again put himself in such a vulnerable position as loving another human being. The universe had given them Milly.

'Isn't she beautiful?' Sadie said, her eyes on the baby, her expression brimming with maternal love that flooded his body with relief.

He remembered Karolina looking at Miko that way.

Roman nodded, mutely, unable to take his

burning eyes off his tiny daughter, who looked just like Miko at the same age—same wispy soft dark hair, same cute little nose, same dimpled chin.

'She looks like her brother,' he choked out, his chest lanced with fresh grief as he recalled his beloved son at Milly's age. Miko would have been ten now, a perfect big brother, a fun and responsible role model. 'But she also looks like you.'

When he met Sadie's stare, gratitude and confusion fighting for control of his pulse, there were tears in her beautiful eyes. He cupped her cheek, wiping one away with his thumb.

He needed to stop touching Sadie, his feelings for her only complicating an already fraught situation. But touching her made him feel better, reminded him of their growing emotional connection before the baby bombshell. Reminded him that, even in pain as they'd both been the night they met, their connection had produced something unique and magical.

'I'm sorry, Roman,' she said, blinking. 'If this is too much, that's fine, honestly. I can't imagine what you must be feeling, but I do understand how hard this is for you.'

Roman swallowed, touched by Sadie's maturity and empathy. She could have reacted so differently.

'But I want you to know that, for me…' she put her hand on her chest, over her heart '… Milly is everything. She's a miracle I never thought I would have the chance to experience. She's deeply, deeply loved and always will be.'

She was letting him know that he was free of parental responsibility, if he wanted to continue his rolling-stone lifestyle. Except her impassioned assurances left him restless once more. He still didn't know what he wanted, but none of the scenarios he'd imagined these past few days felt right.

'I want to provide for Milly, financially,' he said, clearing his tight throat. He'd reached that decision almost immediately, his sense of responsibility the one certainty that came easily and painlessly.

Sadie frowned, as if the idea had never once occurred to her. 'That isn't necessary. As you know, I have a secure job, so she will want for nothing.'

Roman compressed his mouth, picking up on Sadie's slightly defensive tone of voice. 'It's necessary to me to share the responsibility. We made her together, after all.'

Walking away without providing for the daughter they'd made had never once crossed his mind.

'Okay…' Sadie nodded warily. 'If you want.'

There was that nebulous word again, want.

'Life isn't always about having what you want, is it?' he said, glancing at the baby. They both understood that. But financial support was the one practical thing he could do immediately, without ripping open the scabs on his battle-scarred heart.

Roman turned over his phone, keeping an eye on the time. The screen lit up and Sadie saw the background image.

'Is that Miko?' she asked, her curiosity natural after the things they'd shared.

Roman nodded, despite the stab of pain he always experienced on seeing his favourite photo of Karolina and Miko, unlocking his phone and passing it over.

'Karolina had just tickled Miko when I captured that shot,' he said, watching Sadie stare at the phone, her eyes wide, a soft smile playing on her lips. Of course he was biased, but his son's laughter and joy would surely make anyone smile.

'He looked like a mini version of you,' she whispered in awe, 'but with his mother's fair hair.'

'It was dark when he was a baby, just like Milly.' Roman glanced once more at his sleeping daughter, emotions slamming into him.

Could he do this again? Be the kind of father this tiny innocent girl deserved? What if he tried and failed, let her down the way he'd failed Miko? But could he seriously walk away from his daughter, when he was already in love with her, just knowing that she existed?

Sadie handed back the phone and he checked the time with a wince.

'I need to go. I'm due in clinic.'

'Of course. Will you...be okay?'

Roman nodded automatically, still too awed by the turn of events and overwhelmed by his conflicted feelings to describe himself as *okay*. Would he ever be okay again now that there was Milly? Parenthood brought responsibility. Fears for a child's safety and well-being.

He pocketed his phone, the image of Miko's smile fresh in his mind. Of course the joys of being a parent, the uncontrollable love, outweighed the fears and doubts tenfold.

'I'll call you,' he said, standing and resting his hand on Sadie's shoulder. 'I know we need to talk, but I'm on call tonight.'

He wished he could offer some sort of reassurance beyond financial aid.

Sadie nodded, squeezed his fingers. 'When you're ready, I'll be here.'

The trouble was, his greatest fear of all was, that he might never be ready to be the kind of father that Milly deserved. He'd been there once before and a big part of him believed that he'd somehow failed his son, Miko.

He was a doctor, the boy's father. He should have been there for him in his moment of greatest need. It was irrational, but that didn't make it less visceral or devastating. Until he'd reconciled that part of his grief, until he had some clarity on the correct course, he wouldn't fail anyone else.

The following evening, Sadie was about to leave the emergency department after admitting her final patient of the day, a seven-year-old with suspected appendicitis, when an A and E nurse called her to assess a newly arrived emergency.

'Nine-month-old with possible foreign body ingestion in Resus,' the nurse said, handing Sadie the ambulance summary.

Sadie hurried into the resuscitation room, where the most serious cases presenting to the emergency department were assessed. Choking was one of the hazards designed to terrify all parents, so Sadie's heart went out to the concerned pair as she introduced herself.

Sam, the baby, was grizzling and drooling, a distinct high-pitched sound, known as stridor, coming from his throat on every inhaled breath.

'I think there may be an object stuck in Sam's throat,' she explained after taking a brief history from the parents, who hadn't seen the baby swallow anything.

Sadie reached for her stethoscope and listened to the boy's lungs and looked inside his mouth.

'It could be lodged either at the top of his trachea or his oesophagus, the tube to his stomach.' She kept her voice even, while urgency pounded through her blood.

'Most swallowed objects pass through the gut without intervention,' she continued, 'but I don't think this one is going to pass on its own. It's stuck there, and is affecting Sam's breathing. So I'm going to run some tests.'

While the worried parents tried to soothe Sam, Sadie ordered an urgent chest X-ray and paged the on-call surgical registrar. If the object wasn't removed quickly, it could cause tissue damage and, in return, scarring, leaving baby Sam with lifelong complications.

'I'm going to ask my surgical colleagues to take a look at Sam,' she explained to the parents, her mind turning to Milly, who was only a few months younger than this baby. 'It may be that he requires a small procedure under sedation to look into the throat and remove whatever is lodged there.'

Sam's parents appeared understandably horrified. Sadie left them with the ED nurse, who was trying with infinite patience to encourage Sam to wear an oxygen nasal cannula.

She was examining the chest X-ray when Roman walked in.

'What have we got?' he asked, shooting her that smile that shot her pulse through the roof.

He paused beside her, peering over her shoulder at the screen, the hint of his cologne tickling her senses. Unfair memories bombarded her: the scent of his skin, the delirious passion of his kisses, the feel of his body moving inside hers.

Her entire body reacted with goosebumps; she was so pleased to see him.

'Ah, foreign object?' he said, as if completely unmoved by Sadie's proximity, whereas she was engulfed in flames at his casual closeness. 'Some sort of plastic block, I'd guess.'

'That's what I was thinking,' she agreed, leaning away for self-preservation. 'Shouldn't you have left by now? You were on call last night.'

She noted the fatigue around his eyes, the dishevelled mop of his hair, his crumpled scrubs. Was he hiding out from his personal life at work? He'd once admitted workaholic tendencies. But what did that mean for Milly and their...situation? Perhaps he hadn't given it any thought.

'I was about to head out,' he said, 'but my registrar is busy, so I said I'd come down and see what's going on.' He pinned her with his eye contact. 'Thanks for caring.'

'Any time,' Sadie said, flustered because there seemed to be a new resolve about him tonight, and it was crazy sexy.

'Come on. Let's sort out this baby.' Without further discussion, he ducked through the curtains where Sam and his parents sat, with Sadie on his heels.

The baby really didn't want to wear the nasal oxygen cannula, constantly grabbing at his face to pull it away. He took one look at Roman, the newest arrival in a long line of scary strangers, and burst into pitiful tears.

Taking the slight in his stride, Roman introduced himself to Sam's concerned parents. 'My name is Dr Ježek. Dr Barnes has correctly identified a foreign object stuck in Sam's throat.'

Without missing a beat, he handed a fractious Sam his phone and the baby instantly calmed, distracted by the lit-up screen.

Sadie sighed with longing. He was so good at his job. He was such a natural with kids and on the parents' wavelength. For what must have been the thousandth time since they'd reconnected, she imagined what kind of father he would make to their baby girl, if only he could overcome his grief.

But he might never be ready for more and she would have to be okay with that.

'We need to get whatever it is out before it can cause any damage, okay?' Roman asked with the kind of calm assurance that was instantly soothing.

The parents nodded in unison.

Glancing at Sadie to include her in the process, he went on. 'We'll just give Sam a light sedation. Through here.' He indicated the butterfly IV Sadie had already inserted into the baby's arm. 'Dr Barnes and I will then place an endoscope, a small telescope-like tube, into Sam's throat and, fingers crossed, we can grab hold of whatever it is and pull it out. Any questions?'

The couple shook their heads, appearing awed and relieved by Roman's command of the situation.

Sadie exhaled, trying to settle the admiring flutter in her chest. The way he referenced Sadie, including her in the decision-making process, put them once more on the same team.

While Roman asked Sam's dad to sign the consent for the procedure, Sadie injected the IV with a mild dose of sedative.

'You're welcome to stay with Sam if you want,' Sadie said to the grown-ups as the baby lolled drowsily in his father's arms, 'but he'll be asleep and won't really know if you're here. You might find the procedure distressing to watch, so if you prefer to wait in the family room, one of us will come and get you as soon as it's over.'

Agreeing, they laid Sam on the bed, where the nurse adjusted his nasal oxygen cannula and attached a pulse oximeter to monitor his blood oxygen saturations.

With the parents departed, Roman stepped close and cast Sadie a discreet look. 'Any psychosocial concerns?' he asked, pulling on gloves and preparing the endoscope.

It was a sad fact of the job, but paediatricians and those working with children had to constantly be aware of neglect or non-accidental injury in the children they treated.

Sadie shook her head. 'He has an older brother,' she said, donning her own gloves. 'Sam most likely got hold of a stray toy left on the floor.'

For a moment they stared at each other, silently communicating understanding and compassion because they too were parents. Or perhaps that was just in Sadie's head. Wishful thinking.

'Okay. Let's do this,' he said, lightly touching Sadie's arm and directing her to stand at his side so they could both see the screen where the digital images from the endoscope would be displayed.

With a mouthpiece inserted, Roman passed

the flexible tube into Sam's throat, while Sadie closely monitored the baby's breathing.

'There it is,' Roman said, indicating the image on the screen, relief in the glance he flicked Sadie. 'Just at the top of the oesophagus.'

'You're right. It is a plastic block.'

'Right, let's test my fishing skills,' Roman said, extending the tiny forceps at the end of the endoscope to grasp hold of the piece of plastic.

It took several attempts, but when Roman managed to snare the object, Sadie exhaled in relief.

'I know,' he said, flicking her a conspiratorial smile that made her feel as if she'd known him for years, not weeks. 'For a minute there I thought I might need to take this little guy to Theatre. No one wants that.'

With the object retrieved and the endoscope withdrawn, Roman peeled off his gloves and addressed one of the nurses. 'Can you please let Mum and Dad know that everything went smoothly? We'll just admit Sam for observation tonight.'

He looked down at the peacefully sleeping baby, who was breathing easy now that the obstruction had been removed.

Sadie watched in wonder as Roman reached out and gently stroked the baby's head, murmuring something in Czech.

Sadie froze, mesmerised by the telling gesture.

Roman might be a busy surgeon, a breed known for their arrogance, but he truly cared about his patients and their families.

He looked up and their eyes locked.

Sadie's heartbeat whooshed in her ears. He was so competent and compelling. So intelligent and supportive. Every time they worked together she felt their connection growing stronger. At the hospital, they trusted each other and there was a big part of Sadie that craved the same connection in their personal lives, where nothing was certain.

He eyed her sheepishly. 'What?' he asked, tossing his balled-up gloves in the nearby bin.

'Nothing,' Sadie said, fighting the urge to fling herself into his arms and tell him how wonderful he was, beg him to want her with the same all-encompassing desire.

'Are you heading home now?' he asked as they finished up the paperwork on Sam's admission. 'I hoped we could talk.'

His stare carried that vulnerability she wanted to soothe away.

'Yes. I'm done for the day.' Nervous tension coiled in Sadie's belly as they left the emergency department side by side. She didn't want to talk. She wanted to quiet all the doubts in her head with the mind-numbing passion they shared.

'You won't be surprised to hear that I've been

thinking,' he started, holding open a door for Sadie to pass through as they headed for the staff locker rooms. 'And I've decided that I need to try and be a part of Milly's life.'

Sadie's step faltered, her heart leaping in her chest as if she'd just walked into a brick wall. 'Roman, you don't have to rush into any decisions. There's absolutely no pressure from my end.'

It was only yesterday that he'd met Milly in person. Why had he changed his mind so quickly when, in the café, he'd been so hesitant and cautious?

'I know there's no pressure from you,' he said, scanning his security pass to unlock the doors to the changing rooms, 'but this comes from in here.' He pressed his balled-up hand to the centre of his chest, his voice impassioned.

The doors closed behind them, he stepped close and gripped her arms above the elbows. 'I see babies every day at work, even in passing around the hospital, and all I can do is think about my baby, Milly.'

His stare searched Sadie's, imploring. 'I'm walking around feeling like something's not right, as if I've left the oven on at home or forgotten to take my passport to the airport, or I'm missing a surgical clamp in Theatre and the patient is already back on the ward.'

Sadie swallowed, empathy an ache in her chest. 'I can understand that.'

Of course she could. If the situation were reversed, if she had a daughter she'd never met, she wouldn't be able to stay away for one day. But their situations were different. For Roman, Milly's existence also represented painful reminders.

Except his sudden change of heart left fear trickling through her veins.

'Take Sam, for example,' he rushed on. 'Back there, I couldn't stop imagining how I'd feel if it was Milly who needed an operation or emergency treatment. You must sometimes feel that too?'

She nodded, mutely, because she'd been thinking exactly that. But Roman had been through the worst thing any parent could experience. He might never be ready to be fully open. She didn't want hasty promises she'd struggle to trust.

As if reading her mind, he continued. 'I'm still not making any big promises,' he said with heart-rending sincerity, 'but the past few days have shown me that I need to meet my daughter properly, to try and get to know her, and somehow make up for the time I've already missed.'

As if he sensed the chills of doubt that crept up Sadie's spine, he reached for her hand, his touch adding to her confusion. 'What do you think?'

Sadie swallowed the lump of fear in her throat.

How could she deny him anything when she agreed? When she felt closer to him with each passing day? When Milly deserved a father?

Except she'd been so wrong about Mark that she still struggled to trust her instincts.

She hated future-gazing and she didn't want to start now. But surely if they were careful, if she could keep a lid on her desires for him, they could take things slowly and apply the same trust to their personal lives as they practised at work.

Desperately trying to ignore the flicker of excitement in his eyes, she brought her hands up and gripped his arms. 'I think we should take things slowly.'

She would never keep Roman from his daughter, but this about-face left her...unsettled. 'After all, you're going to Ireland in a couple of weeks.'

A small frown pinched his brows.

But it was a good reminder for them both to proceed with caution. No matter how close she felt towards him, he was still leaving London. Trusting him with the most precious thing in her world, Milly, meant trusting her instincts and taking a giant leap of faith, something that had gone badly for her in the past.

'Of course, I want you and Milly to know each other,' Sadie said, taking that leap for her daughter's sake. And for Roman. 'So if you're sure you're ready...'

Tugging her into his arms, Roman kissed the top of her head. 'Thank you. I agree; we'll take it one day at a time.'

Sadie nodded against his chest as he continued to hold her, turned on by his touch, conflicted by his gratitude and restraint. Her head felt full of cotton wool, the longing for it to work warring with her maternal protective urges for her darling baby.

And something darker—the demands of her own tangled needs.

But with so much else going on, that would have to be the last thing on her mind.

'That being said—' he pulled back, his stare vulnerable '—how would you feel about an outing tomorrow, just the three of us? Perhaps we could take Milly to the zoo?'

He looked so hopeful, so exposed, Sadie nodded, her smile feeble. 'That sounds nice.'

His delighted expression burned Sadie's eyes. How could she deny him when she'd always hoped that he'd want to be a part of Milly's life? But how would she spend time with him away from work and keep him at arm's length, emotionally and physically, so she could follow her own edict and take things one day at a time?

CHAPTER NINE

THEY'D ARRANGED TO meet just inside the main entrance of the zoo, near the aquarium. The minute Roman spied Sadie pushing Milly's buggy, he breathed a relieved sigh, his heart pounding with excitement.

He had no idea how today would unfold, but it was time to come to terms with the fact that he and Sadie had made a beautiful baby together.

He couldn't stay away any longer.

He walked towards them, his stare greedily taking in Milly, who was awake, wearing a tiny woollen hat and covered in a blanket. Awestruck by her big blue eyes, he dragged in a lungful of chilly air, braced against the waves of feelings almost knocking him off his feet.

Shocking him the most was the instant love, some visceral protective part of him springing to life. But it wasn't strong enough to completely dispel the trickle of fear tightening his gut or the hot stabs of guilt between his ribs.

'Have you been waiting long?' Sadie asked, breathless, pausing to scrutinise his expression in that caring way of hers.

'Not long,' Roman lied, leaning in to press a kiss to her cold cheek, without hesitation now that they were away from the hospital. He'd arrived way too early, nerves and anticipation shrinking the walls of his one-bedroom flat in the hospital accommodation complex.

He took Sadie's hand and gazed down at the baby, his stare compulsively drawn to his daughter. 'Thanks for agreeing to this.'

Sadie smiled, squeezed his hand, enabling him to draw a decent breath. 'How are you doing? Big day.'

'I'm nervous,' Roman admitted, ashamed, but wanting to be honest.

She nodded in agreement, her beautiful eyes soft with compassion. 'We'll take it slow, together.'

Touched that this amazing woman understood him so well, he held out the small gift he'd brought. 'This is for Milly. Open it later— It's cold out here.'

Sadie took the gift and tucked it into her bag as Roman held open the door to the aquarium exhibits. 'Let's go look at some fish.'

Once inside the aquarium building, Sadie parked up the buggy and unstrapped Milly, removing her hat. Static electricity raised her fine downy hair so it stood on end. Sadie laughed and Milly smiled, oblivious to what was funny.

Roman's heart jolted as if he'd been electrocuted.

Watching Sadie smile at their daughter, seeing her unbridled love and joy and awe for the baby they'd made together… A beautiful moment of maternal love he would try to hold onto for ever. A moment like a thousand others he'd lived with Karolina and Miko.

His chest ached as he remembered the good times, his euphoria tainted with guilt and grief because he'd had these chances before.

As Sadie wandered the three-hundred-and-sixty-degree tank filled with coral and colourful tropical fish, holding Milly up to the glass to point out the brightly contrasted creatures, Roman trailed along, watching their breathtaking interactions with wonder.

Did he deserve a second shot at being a father when there was a part of him, an irrational, primitive part, that felt somehow responsible for the deaths of his family? He'd spent years torturing himself with unanswerable questions. What if he'd been driving the car that night instead of being at work? What if he'd been with them, able to help in a medical capacity? What if they'd all stayed home, safe and sound?

How had he imagined he would be able to keep his emotions in check today, one glimpse of his daughter's smile leaving him raw and exposed?

Shoving those thoughts aside—it wasn't fair to Milly—Roman watched his daughter jerk her arms and legs with excitement, her gaze following the movements of the fish swimming past.

Sadie smiled and pointed and made fish faces, her animation contagious, glancing over at him to include him in the moment.

A wild storm of longing and admiration spun inside him like a hurricane. Being around his daughter was wonderful and heart-wrenching. Watching Sadie mother their child made him want her even more. He already knew that she was good with children from work. But this was different.

This was *their* child.

Clearing his dry throat, Roman clung to a distraction. 'What have you told people about Milly's father?'

Sadie stiffened, her delighted smile for Milly fading. 'Umm…not much. My sister knows about you, obviously,' she said, apologetically. 'But no one at work knows, if that's what you're worried about.'

Roman shrugged, some deeply rooted primal imperative demanding the world knew that he'd fathered this beautiful baby. 'I'm not worried, just curious.'

How he and Sadie met was their business. They weren't a couple. And she clearly didn't want anyone at work to know that he was Milly's father.

'Have *you* told anyone?' Sadie asked warily.

Roman nodded. 'Just my parents and my brothers and sister.'

'How many siblings do you have?'

'Five. I come from a big family.'

'Five?' Sadie said, her eyes wide with shock.

He smiled, changing the subject because, one day, he'd like Milly to meet her Czech family, but they'd agreed to take each day at a time. 'And the baby is thriving? Growing, eating, sleeping?'

His hands itched to hold Milly, the bonding instinct primal.

Sadie smiled up at him, the baby happy in her arms. 'She's perfect and doing everything she should be doing.'

Roman swallowed the lump in his throat; she was perfect.

'Would you like to hold her?' Sadie asked, her expression relaxed and encouraging.

'Yes,' he said, instinctively, holding out his arms. His heart pounded, but he needed to feel the baby's weight in his arms, to feel her tiny heartbeat and know that she was real.

His daughter.

Sadie handed over Milly with a bright smile that told the baby she was safe with this stranger.

Roman gripped the precious bundle, dipping his head to catch the warm baby scent of her. He tried to commit it to memory, his eyes closing on a wave of primitive feelings: innate recognition, fierce protective instincts, a surge of love.

'It's okay,' Sadie said, talking to Milly in a reassuring voice, her arm coming around his back, enclosing the three of them in a bubble of intimacy.

For an unguarded moment, Roman saw a flash of what might have been, imagined the three of them as a family. But he'd already had that.

A frisson of panic slithered down his spine.

Was he capable of being a proper father again? The idea of loving another child laced his blood with fear that he'd forget Miko. But now that he'd met her, held her, recognised her, the doubt that he might be too broken to love his innocent daughter didn't bear thinking about. With each passing day since he'd discovered her existence, the urgency to know her, to ensure she was safe and happy, to protect and care for her had taken over.

'*Poklad...*' he whispered, pressing a soft kiss to the top of Milly's head.

'What does that mean?' Sadie asked, resting

her head on his arm, as if she understood he needed her close.

'I called her *treasure*. It's a Czech term of endearment.' His gaze was drawn to Sadie's soft smile, her embrace slotting a piece of him back into place.

'She is precious.' Sadie nodded, staring deep into his eyes.

This woman had brought his broken spirit solace, first in Vienna, when their night of passion had reminded him that he was capable of feeling something positive and light-hearted, and again when she'd turned his world upside down with news of his daughter.

'Thank you,' he whispered, trying to untangle his gratitude from the other feelings he had for Sadie.

'Why are you thanking me?' she said, her eyes swimming with emotion and flickers of desire he was so relieved to see.

'For making such a beautiful baby,' he said in a low voice, thick with reverence. 'For giving me time to come to terms with the news. For sharing her with me.'

His voice broke on the last word.

Sadie gripped his waist tighter. 'You're welcome. I'm sorry that you missed out on her first two months.'

He cast her a sad smile. 'Time I missed because I made a stupid decision to seduce a sexy stranger without getting her name and number.'

Sadie stared, her body warm against his. It would be so easy, almost second nature to cup her face close for a kiss. Part of him was desperate to explore their chemistry, their growing connection, the rest of him certain they should set that aside and focus all their energy on Milly.

'She seduced you too,' Sadie whispered, clearly battling a similar dilemma.

Then something amazing happened. Milly smiled, first at Sadie, waving her little fist, and then up at Roman.

He gasped, something inside him cracking open, letting in a shaft of light.

He had no idea if he'd be able to do fatherhood a second time, but he wouldn't waste the amazing chance he'd been given to be a member of this little family. Milly deserved a father willing to make a fresh start. She deserved to have as much stability and love and opportunity as he'd lavished on Miko.

The question was, could he put down the roots he'd avoided for so long when he was so out of practice? And what would those roots represent for him and Sadie? Constant temptation or the foundations of something neither of them expected?

* * *

Roman placed a tray on the table and took the seat next to Sadie in the zoo's Forest Café. 'I brought you water as well as tea. Nursing mothers need to stay hydrated, as you know.'

'Thank you.' Sadie swallowed the lump the size of a rock in her throat, high from the emotions of the day.

Spending time with Roman away from work was terrifyingly easy, their connection back on track.

After a few hesitant moments, he'd embraced Milly with wonder and tenderness that had been hard to watch. Holding her as if she was precious, staring at her funny baby faces and nonsensical gurgles with awe, whispering to her in Czech.

How could Sadie be expected to stay immune to such exhilarating moments of father and daughter bonding? To stay immune to Roman the doting father?

Milly finished her feed, and unlike a few weeks ago, when she would usually fall asleep afterwards, now she was more intent on taking in all the new sights and sounds.

'You drink and I'll get her wind up,' Roman said, reaching for the muslin square Sadie kept handy for milky burps.

Telling herself she was simply awash with love hormones from nursing their daughter, Sadie handed the baby over, braced once more for the sight of Roman holding Milly, staring down at her with that breathtaking smile on his face.

'I'm hogging her, aren't I?' he said, unapologetically cuddling her close.

His eagerness made Sadie's eyes smart. 'It's okay; she's waited a long time to meet you.'

Considering that a few days ago she'd been scared Roman would disown their daughter, his reaction to being properly introduced to their daughter had squashed many of Sadie's doubts—her concern for Roman's grieving process and her fear of introducing her precious Milly to a stranger.

They stared at each other over the daughter they'd made together. Just as they'd been doing all morning, feelings rushed Sadie, wave after wave of desire for this wonderful man, a new level of contentment, stronger than anything she'd experienced before. Every time he'd looked at her today, she'd seen admiration, as if he saw Sadie in a whole new light. A woman with whom he'd created a life.

Heady stuff for someone already turned on by his hand-holding, moved by his small acts of thoughtfulness, and overcome by the way he seemed to have welcomed her beloved Milly into his heart.

Was this how it felt when children brought couples closer?

Except she and Roman weren't a couple and never would be.

Roman would always be in love with another woman, and Sadie had trust issues and insecurities. He came from a big family and Milly was likely to be Sadie's only child. He moved around to avoid the pain of losing his family, and, after years of yearning but accepting that she might never have a baby, Sadie couldn't bear to think of sharing Milly in some complex custody arrangement. But realistically, if Roman intended to stay in his daughter's life, that was exactly what awaited the three of them.

Unless his itchy feet, the lure of that rolling-stone lifestyle of his, would eventually outweigh his desire to change nappies.

In an attempt to distract her from the panic hijacking her pulse, Sadie retrieved the gift from Milly's nappy bag. 'Can I open this now?'

She didn't want to consider what *the future* entailed for them now that Roman wanted to be a part of Milly's life.

'Of course.' He looked up from winding Milly, turning his adoring expression on Sadie with a smile.

She couldn't get carried away by one successful outing. It was early days. Plenty of time for

Roman to change his mind about wanting Milly in his life.

Inside the wrapping was a charming wooden pull-along toy in the shape of a duck. The minute the baby saw the bright yellow beak she grasped for it.

'Wooden toys are traditional in the Czech Republic,' Roman explained, sliding closer to Sadie so their thighs touched. 'I know she won't use it for a while, but I wanted her to have something from the oldest toy shop in Prague.'

'It's beautiful,' Sadie whispered, the flicker of pain dimming his eyes telling her that he'd probably shopped there for Miko, too. 'She'll treasure it.'

'She's amazing, Sadie,' he said, stroking the soft curls at the nape of Milly's neck.

'I know,' she managed to choke out, the sight of this sexy, competent and intelligent man as a gentle and nurturing father almost too much for her poor weak and hormone-ridden body to endure.

Spending time as a family, while wonderful for Milly and Roman, was messing with Sadie's head. She didn't want to be hurt.

'I've been thinking,' she said. 'I know you didn't have a say in naming Milly, so if you want to add a middle name, perhaps something Czech, we can officially alter her birth certificate.'

'I'd like that.' His smile of gratitude spurred her on.

'Also, I wonder if you could send me a picture of Miko. I'd like to put a framed photo in Milly's room, so I can tell her about her big brother as she grows.'

'Of course.' His stare filled with stormy emotions as he reached out and cupped her face, his thumb gliding along her cheekbone. 'You're a special person, Sadie, and a wonderful mother.'

His eyes bored into hers, shutting out the people around them. 'I know we're taking one day at a time, but I hoped you might one day bring Milly to Prague. My family would love to meet her.'

'Of course… I hadn't thought of that, but of course they want to meet her…'

Fear fizzed in her veins. Roman wanted to proudly introduce his daughter to the Czech side of her family. Maybe when she was older, the visits wouldn't include Sadie at all.

The idea of Roman and Milly spending time without her pinched at Sadie's stomach. But she'd need to get used to that. The future held shared custody, separate holidays and Christmas Days and birthdays where they'd need to find some fair way of sharing their daughter.

No wonder she was reluctant to think too far ahead. The future was horribly uncertain.

'The idea unsettles you,' he said, his stare full of understanding. 'You've been used to having Milly all to yourself.'

Sadie shook her head. 'It's not that. I just don't like planning too far ahead. Life is…unpredictable, as you know, and I try to live in the moment rather than freak myself out with scary what ifs.'

When she'd first met Mark, he'd seemed too wonderful to be true. And as it had turned out, she'd been right.

'Okay,' he said, not pushing, but taking her hand.

Sadie squirmed, forcing herself to open up because Roman deserved more of an explanation. 'It's a habit that began when I received my infertility diagnosis, but my ex, Mark, was a very demonstrative person, always making grand romantic gestures, or voicing big plans for our future as a couple. *"When we get married, we can go to Bali for our honeymoon…" "If we buy this two-bedroom flat in Islington, in three years we'll be able to afford to upgrade to a bigger home in Hampstead…" "When we retire, we could move to Spain…"'*

She glanced away from the compassion in Roman's eyes, way out of her comfort zone.

'Over the years we were together, he drew me into his dreams, made me believe that our future was out there waiting for us, full of hope and optimism even though I was unlikely to ever have my greatest wish: a baby of my own.'

Roman tensed at her side, his face slashed with a harsh frown.

'He'd said that we'd be happy even if it was just the two of us, and I believed him, felt lucky to have such a wonderful partner in my life, someone who accepted me just the way I am. Then one day,' she said, taking comfort from his touch, 'he came home from work and told me he was leaving me, just like that. While we'd been making plans to get engaged, to have a spring wedding and that honeymoon in Bali, he'd also been making plans with another woman. A woman from work he'd been sleeping with for three months. A woman he'd got pregnant. She was giving him the one thing I couldn't, so he chose her over me.'

'I'm sorry that you were so badly let down,' Roman said, his stare searching hers.

'I'm not the only person to have ever been cheated on,' Sadie said, a little numb and a whole lot uncertain how her instincts had been so wrong where Mark was concerned. 'And I was mostly angry that he used me as a place holder until someone better came along. That, when it came to the crunch, he'd lied: my infertility *did* matter.'

'People cheat for many complex reasons,' Roman said, defensive on her behalf. 'It was about him, not you.'

'I know.' Sadie shrugged. But she had allowed herself to be sucked into Mark's dreams, the pretty promises and the pictures they'd painted. 'I was long over him the night we met in Vienna. I'm well shot of a shallow person who would lie and cheat.'

But her ability to trust her judgement still felt bruised, some small part of her deep inside still doubting that she'd ever be good enough for another relationship.

Roman tilted his head in that way of his, seeing her too clearly. 'You deserve so much more than a man like that. You're kind and caring and funny and smart. You deserve someone who—'

As if he'd had an unpleasant thought, he broke off abruptly.

Was he jealous of this fictional future man? Did he hate the idea of someone else helping to raise their daughter? Or was it simply that he'd been about to admit aloud that the man she deserved could never be him.

Fortunately, Milly started to grizzle, rubbing at her eyes and giving Sadie a legitimate reason to shy away from the moment of vulnerability.

'Oh—it's nap time. We should probably go.' Sadie wrestled Milly into her coat and hat, and Roman tucked her into the buggy, covering her with a blanket.

By the time they'd walked to the Camden

Town Tube station, the baby was fast asleep. As they were headed in different directions, Sadie paused inside to say goodbye.

'Thank you for today, Sadie,' Roman said, glancing down at a sleeping Milly. 'I know we still have a lot to figure out, but I appreciate your patience with me.'

He looked frozen, as if he couldn't bring himself to walk away from his baby, now that they'd met.

Sadie blinked, her eyes stinging. 'We don't have to figure everything out. One day at a time, remember.'

Roman nodded, hesitating as if he had more to say.

'Will you be okay?' she asked, her chest aching with compassion.

He nodded once, decisive. But he didn't move, only scoured her face for what felt like hours, returning time and again to her mouth.

She was reminded of that first day, when they'd been stuck in the ward office together, the lock jammed. Part of her had been desperate to flee and the other part unable to move, waiting for his kiss. Except she knew him so much better now, the sexual tension between them fierce and unrelenting now that they had the most important thing in the world in common: a child.

Only it was because of that child that they needed to be, oh, so careful.

Perhaps deciding that he could delay no longer, Roman cast one last look at the baby and swooped close, gripping Sadie's arm and pressing a swift kiss to her cheek.

There was a split second where time seemed suspended. Sadie considered turning her head so their lips would connect. But their chemistry was too strong. She wanted him too badly. If she kissed him now, she'd invite him home. They'd end up in bed.

But it had been an emotional day, for both of them.

Stepping back, she retreated to safety. 'I'll see you tomorrow, at work.'

Scanning her travel card, she pushed the buggy through the accessible barrier, without looking back, her heart and her stomach a knotted mess.

It would be so easy to allow her desire for Roman to rule her head. They were grown adults each with valid reasons for keeping their attraction in check. It was exhilarating to believe that neither of them would allow anything to get in the way of what was best for their baby. That they could indulge their physical connection without consequence.

Except Milly was living proof that repercussions could sneak up on you.

CHAPTER TEN

'SO THE GOOD news is that you're doing so well,' Roman told Josh, resting a hand on the boy's shoulder, 'that we can take out the chest drain and make you more comfortable.'

Josh gave a hesitant smile, his eyes bright with excitement, a sign that he was clearly on the mend, and Roman glanced at Sadie for confirmation.

'We can remove it this morning.' Sadie nodded, making a note in Josh's file while Roman answered a couple of questions from his parents.

Roman forced himself to look away.

Ever since the trip to the zoo two days ago, he hadn't been able to stop thinking about Sadie and Milly. Sadie's devotion to their adorable daughter had boosted his attraction to her tenfold. Motherhood brought out new and rousing aspects of her personality. He lived for the glimpses of her at work. Craved her texts and the pictures she sent of her and Milly together. Even now, with her standing right next to him, he missed their connection.

But just because they were parents who shared potent chemistry, didn't mean a relationship between him and Sadie should be full steam ahead. As it was, he was reeling from a crash refresher course on how to be a father.

His daughter… He'd so easily fallen in love with his baby; he'd had little choice. Milly gave him a reason to open his eyes in the morning, already an undeniable and permanent piece of his heart.

After the accident, he'd embraced his solitary existence. But he hadn't realised how much he'd missed simple everyday things. Family things. Outings. But now that there was Milly to consider, the things he'd lived without seemed important once more. His world had opened up. All the things he wanted to show Milly. All things they could do together. All the moments he would cherish and never take for granted leaving him full of restless excitement he hadn't felt for many years.

And it was all down to Sadie, the woman who had given their daughter life, a passionate, caring woman who'd been badly hurt.

Could the three of them be a family, his second? Was he capable of being the father he needed to be while also trying to build a relationship? Would Sadie even want that after her past experiences?

Because if it all went wrong, he could lose everything.

'Can I leave you to remove the drain?' he asked as they left Josh's bedside, wishing they were anywhere else but at work.

The more time he spent with Sadie, the harder it was becoming to separate the instant love he felt for Milly from the admiration, respect and gratitude he felt for Sadie.

And lust, don't forget lust.

But that didn't mean he was ready to risk his heart in a romantic way.

'Of course. I'll see to it.' She looked up at him, questions in her beautiful eyes.

She wanted to know if he was okay after meeting Milly. Could he explain the disorientating collision of his painful past and this unexpected present he'd experienced meeting his baby girl. How mesmerised he'd been by the maternal love he saw between Sadie and Milly because he'd witnessed the same between Karolina and Miko. How holding Milly, inhaling her scent and touching her baby soft skin, somehow made his memories of Miko more vivid. How Sadie's thoughtfulness when she'd asked for a picture of his son had almost undone him.

'I miss her,' he whispered, knowing that Sadie would understand who he meant. 'Is she okay?'

The ward was busy; they had no privacy, and he needed to go to Theatre. Only he couldn't bring himself to walk away.

'She's good.' Sadie's smile lit her eyes with tenderness. 'Why don't you come over after work? We can chat about the auction while we bath her together. You can read a bedtime story.'

Pain lanced his chest, bittersweet. 'I'd love that.'

How many bath or story times had he shared with Miko? Not enough. He wouldn't take the opportunity to participate in such a simple everyday moment with his daughter for granted. But the restlessness he'd felt since he'd learned of Milly's existence, bloomed anew.

If he was struggling to go a couple of days without seeing Milly, how would he endure weeks or even months apart? His next locum position in Ireland loomed. How could he contemplate moving away when he'd only just begun to know his daughter? How could he miss another second of her precious life?

'You're hesitant,' Sadie remarked with a frown.

He wanted to tell her all his fears and reservations, but he didn't want to scare her after the things she'd told him about her past. Sadie had understandable trust issues and he couldn't make her any promises while he was figuring out how he could be everything he needed to be: doctor, father, lover.

It was better to make a plan, find a way he could be in his daughter's life first, take one day at a time.

The need to have his uncertainties mapped out beat at him anew. He wanted to know Sadie's views on him having regular visitation or even shared custody of Milly. He needed to voice his thoughts on relocating permanently to London to watch his daughter grow up. He hated the idea of Milly being shipped overseas for her school holidays to visit Roman wherever he was working, and he wanted to know how Sadie saw co-parenting working for them.

Only now wasn't the time to thrash out the details.

More pressing was exactly how he would spend more time with his daughter and not want Sadie.

But acting on those desires could undo the fragile ties of their tiny new family.

'Only because it's hard to be around you and not be…distracted.' His gaze sought the temptation of her lips. She needed to understand that their furious chemistry hadn't gone away. If anything, it was stronger.

'Oh.' She flushed, smiled. 'Do you want to risk it?'

He nodded, wishing he could touch her, wondering for the millionth time why he was fighting his attraction so hard. 'I think we should talk about it. Later? I need to go.'

'I'll text you my address.'

Because he could delay no longer, he turned to leave, his hand deliberately brushing hers at her side. It wasn't the contact he craved, but it would need to sustain him for the rest of the day.

As he walked to the operating suites, he dragged in a deep breath. For a man who, until now, had been content to live out of a suitcase, this evening, spending time with his girls, shone like a beacon of golden light he wanted to run towards.

Except every moment he spent with Sadie was a lesson in temptation.

Roman sighed as he scanned himself into the theatre changing rooms. Never in his life had he needed to be more in control of his feelings, which were a confusing mash-up of past and present, grief and joy. Of his new relationship with his daughter, which would prioritise her security and happiness. Of his attraction to a woman who, because they'd created a life together, had overnight gone from temporary lover to a significant and permanent person in his life.

Determined to find that control so that no one—not him, or Sadie or, most importantly, Milly—got hurt, Roman pulled on his scrubs and prepared for a long day.

Milly jerked her arms and legs excitedly, squealing and splashing Roman in the face with bathwater. He laughed, smiling down at their beautiful daughter with delight in his eyes.

'Good shot, Milly,' Sadie said, reaching for a towel to dab at Roman's dripping face. 'She normally soaks me, so I'm glad that you're here.'

'I needed a soaking after a long day,' he said, reaching for some suds and playfully dabbing them on the end of Sadie's nose when she continued to giggle at his expense. 'And I'm glad I'm here too.'

Sadie shuddered with desire; there was nothing playful about the heat in Roman's eyes. She wiped her nose, taking a second to hide behind the towel while she struggled with the arousal leaving her breathless.

'Are we ready to come out?' Sadie asked Milly, splashing her belly with water to make her smile.

She lifted the baby out and handed her to Roman, who was waiting with a warm, fluffy towel to wrap her up. They dried and dressed Milly together, smiling at her funny facial expressions and the triumphant gurgling sounds she made when she managed to grab a handful of Sadie's long hair.

'I've been thinking,' Roman said, his expression falling serious as Sadie buttoned up Milly's sleep suit. 'I'd like Milly to call me Tatínek if that's okay. It's Czech for Daddy.'

Sadie froze, trying to downplay the significance of the moment. The last time he was called that, it would have been by Miko.

'Of course it's okay.' Sadie picked Milly up, looping her other arm around his waist, holding him to let him know that she understood the importance of his request. 'Tatínek it is.'

Choked by the conflicted emotion flitting across his face at her use of the Czech word, Sadie settled on the sofa with Roman at her side.

Roman read Milly's favourite story and then sang a song in Czech.

'An old Czech folk song my grandfather sang to me, that I used to sing to Miko,' he explained, watching Milly latch on for her final feed.

'Do you ever miss home?' Sadie asked, scared to know but also aware that Roman's heritage was Milly's heritage.

He shrugged, entwined his fingers with hers in a gesture that now felt second nature. 'Sometimes,' he said in a quiet voice. 'But I think home isn't a place, a town or a city. It's in here.' He pressed his fist to his chest.

Sadie's own heart thumped at his intensity, at how much she wanted to hold him and chase away the shadows in his eyes. At the fever-pitch of how badly she craved their intimacy.

'That's why I can travel around as a locum and still carry Karolina and Miko with me wherever I go,' he added.

Sadie pressed her lips together, desperate to know if he also planned to carry Milly in his heart when he left for Ireland. But she couldn't bear to ask, because thinking about the future meant admitting that Roman might want Milly in his life, but that didn't mean he wanted a romantic relationship with Sadie.

The future was full of all the important days of Milly's life that Sadie would miss while Roman and Milly and eventually some new woman in Roman's life were together. No matter how much she fantasised that she and Roman might one day be a proper couple, reality intervened.

The minute he'd said he came from a big family, a part of her hope had shrivelled to dust. Roman had probably wanted a large family of his own before tragedy struck. But now that he had Milly, there would be nothing to stop him from filling his heart with the love of more children. With the right woman, of course.

And that wasn't Sadie.

'Mind if I put her down?' Roman asked, taking the baby, who'd fallen asleep after her feed.

'Go for it.' Sadie pasted on a brave face, and flopped back against the sofa cushions as he left the room.

She'd never in a million years have imagined that the commitment-shy man she'd met the night they'd conceived would be such a hands-on, caring and dedicated father. But now that she knew the real Roman, she couldn't have asked for a better *tatínek* for her treasured daughter.

It was a serious aphrodisiac, not that she needed one where Roman was concerned.

He was making it so hard for her to ignore what a special man he was, to hold him at arm's length physically so she could keep her emotional distance from their deepening connection. They spent so much time together that the casual touches, comforting embraces and heated looks were becoming increasingly hard to fight.

But maybe she didn't need to fight so hard. Maybe she could sleep with him, one more time, knowing that by keeping things physical she could trust him not to hurt her.

'She didn't stir,' he said as he rejoined Sadie, looking slightly tired and rumpled, his hair mussed, in a thoroughly arousing way, as if he'd run his fingers through it.

He sat, stretched his arm out along the back of the sofa behind Sadie.

'Thank you,' she said, her eyes locked with his, her throat tight.

'What for?' A small frown pinched his brows together as he regarded her with quiet intensity.

'For being you. For embracing Milly the way you have.' His obvious adoration of their baby combined with his extreme hotness left Sadie dangerously off-kilter. 'I'm so glad you found a space in your heart for our little miracle.'

'How could I not? She's delightful. I'm head over heels.' His expression turned serious but his fingers found the back of her neck, stroking. 'Although don't thank me yet. I think I've forgotten how to do fatherhood. I'll probably get it wrong at some point.'

Sadie shook her head, her body melting at the hypnotic rhythm of his touch. 'I think it's naturally coming back to you. Milly will help you remember.'

'She already is.' He nodded, holding her eye contact so she saw the love for their daughter shining there. 'She's a wonderful blessing, for both of us. Getting to know Milly, reliving all these beautiful everyday moments, is somehow making me also feel closer to Miko.'

Of course every joyful moment he shared with their daughter must remind him of similar moments he'd had with his son. That loving Milly was somehow easing his pain shifted something deep inside Sadie's chest, her bruised heart trying to beat to a new, hopeful rhythm.

Sadie stilled, that same heart thudding. Tonight, they'd bonded deeper over their daughter, but they were also two adults insanely attracted to each other.

'You wanted to talk about the auction?' he said.

'Did I...?' Idiot. Why would she want to bring up the topic of him dating another woman?

Why hadn't she given in to temptation and kissed him as soon as he sat down? They could be naked by now.

'I need to work on your bio,' she said. 'I might need to ask you a few more questions.' She sounded half-hearted at best.

His fingers sliding up to her hairline and then down to the bumps of her vertebrae were driving her crazy. But it stopped her thinking about him on a date with another woman. It stopped her thinking that after the Valentine's fundraiser he'd be moving on to his next locum position.

'You know everything important about me already, Sadie.' His voice was low, seductive, luring her in.

But he was right. She did know the most important things about this man. She knew that he cared about people, including her. She knew that he kept his word. She knew she wanted him.

She'd never stopped wanting him.

'But I want you to know this, too.' As if he saw her deepest fears in her eyes, he cupped her face. 'I know you've been hurt in the past. But I'll do everything in my power to do right by you and Milly.'

Choked by the depth of feeling in his admission, by his vulnerability and the way he included her in his new family, Sadie groaned. 'Roman...'

She was desperate now, his touch lighting up every cell in her body.

She rested her forehead against his. 'We should stop.' It emerged a feeble whisper.

His fingers curled into her hair at the nape of her neck, his breath coming hard. 'I know... I know.'

'I want you.' Her hands found his waist, fisting his T-shirt.

Their breath mingled.

He pulled back, his hands sliding to her shoulders, fingers digging as he fought some epic internal battle. 'Kick me out.'

Sadie shook her head, her heart rate dizzyingly high. 'We just need to be careful.'

He nodded, something in his eyes shifting.

Sadie instinctively knew that he understood

everything she'd left unsaid. That he'd be true to his word. That they would put Milly first.

Roman was different. She could trust him with her body, knowing that, with the exception of their daughter's happiness, their priorities hadn't changed since their first night together. It would just be sex. Amazing, wonderful sex.

Reaching the limit of their endurance together, they pounced. Their lips met in a rush. Eager. Days of longing rendering Sadie wild with desire.

Roman scooped his strong arm around her waist with a groan, hauled her close, chest to chest. Sadie gripped his neck, tunnelled her fingers in his glorious hair, returned his kisses with all her pent-up passion.

Yes, they were parents, but they were also humans. They had their own needs. And right now nothing mattered more than this connection.

'I thought you'd never kiss me,' she panted, straddling Roman's lap.

'I never stopped wanting to,' he said, gripping her hips and tilting his head back against the cushions so Sadie could lean over him, press kisses to his jaw, his neck, his lips, in a thorough exploration. Every sigh and moan swallowed. Every taste savoured.

'You are so sexy.' His hands slid beneath her top, along her ribs, cupping her breasts through her bra. 'Are you sure about this?'

'Absolutely.' She rocked her hips on his lap, grinding his erection between her legs, where she wanted him.

Despite the fact that since they were last intimate she now had stretch marks, Roman made her feel sexy. Wanted. And, oh, how she wanted him in return.

'You've just had a baby,' he said, his thumbs stroking her nipples. 'I don't want to hurt you.'

'You won't.' Sadie collapsed against him, her tongue duelling with his to counter the pleasure he was wreaking with his touch.

He popped the clasp on her bra and raised her top, exposing her breasts with a groan. 'I've thought about this so many times.' He raised her breast and laved her nipple. 'I thought I'd go mad for wanting you.'

'Me too.' Sadie removed her top and tossed it aside, moaning, as his mouth sought her other breast. 'Although we need to be more careful with the condoms, this time…just in case I've become the most fertile woman on the planet.'

Tugging off his shirt, she pressed kisses over his bare chest, goosebumps rising as his chest hair brushed her nipples.

'I'm always careful, but don't worry; this time you've got my number.' He winked, standing up with Sadie in his arms.

Sadie wrapped her arms around his neck,

burying her face there while he strode to her bedroom. As he laid her down on the bed and stood back to admire her partial nakedness, she feared that she might not survive another night as Roman's lover.

Because, aside from his irreparably broken heart, everything else about Roman was dangerously wonderful.

CHAPTER ELEVEN

ROMAN STARED DOWN at Sadie, his breath gusting, the promise he'd made to her still spiralling through his mind. He'd meant it: he'd never hurt Sadie, nor risk hurting Milly. He would always strive to put his new family first. That this amazing, beautiful woman had been so badly let down in the past brought all of his protective urges to the fore.

Plans he'd been mulling over ever since he'd known about Milly solidified. He wasn't sure exactly how yet, but he wanted to be around to help to raise his child, whether or not he and Sadie were romantically involved.

He loved his daughter. He never wanted to miss another bath time.

But tonight was about him and Sadie. And she was right; they would need to be careful. This time, there was more at stake.

'Come here.' Sadie took his hands, drawing him close.

Roman leaned over her and pressed a kiss to her lips, determined to go slow and wring every drop of pleasure from the night. Desire urged him to kiss a path along her neck, pausing when she sighed.

'I want you to know,' he said, kissing her collarbones and the tops of her breasts, 'that because of you, for the first time in years, I feel hopeful.'

Her pupils dilated, her breaths coming faster as she gazed up at him, her stare pleading. 'Roman…'

She tugged the belt loops of his jeans, her hands skimming his ribs, back and shoulders.

But he wanted her to know that she'd turned his life around. 'I haven't slept with anyone else since that night in Vienna.'

For the intervening months, he hadn't questioned why, but now, with her scent on his skin, with her beauty softened by the dim glow of lamplight, with nothing but Sadie in his head, he realised that subconsciously he'd been waiting for someone…extraordinary, like Sadie.

Her eyes widened in surprise.

'I couldn't get you off my mind. It was as if fate had some important reason to draw me back to you.' He stripped off her jeans, skimming his hands up her legs as he lay at her side.

And fate had been right. No matter what the future held for him and Sadie, they would always stay connected.

'I want to make you feel good.' He traced her ribs, cupped her breast, swiped at the nipple with his thumb, watching her reactions. 'Are your breasts tender?' he asked, noticing her shiver.

'No.' She turned to face him, wrapped her arms around his neck, pressing her lips to his. 'Don't treat me like I'm fragile. I want you.'

'I want you too.' It scared him how much; they were so in tune. They'd figure everything else out.

'These need to come off,' Sadie said, her hands working at the buttons of his jeans. Obviously the time for talking was over.

He smiled against her lips, brushing her hair back from her flushed face. 'All in good time.'

She pressed her mouth over his chest while her hands roamed his back, making it hard for him to cling to his sense of control. Roman closed his eyes, momentarily lost in the intensity of her touch, the brush of her nipples, the thud of her heart alongside his, the scrape of her fingernails against his skin.

Unlike the last time they were intimate, now they were so close. For him, it was more than lust and gratitude. More than their shared views and values. More than the way she intuitively understood him. They'd bonded. Over their pasts, over their work, over their daughter.

A deep connection he would always cherish.

Drawing her lips back to his, he kissed her, his thumbs toying with her nipples until they stood erect and she whimpered in pleasure.

'I don't want to hurt you,' he said, 'so tell me to stop if anything is uncomfortable.' He kissed a path down the warm fragrant skin of her neck, across her chest, over her breasts. Embracing the chemistry they'd each fought for so long, he tongued her nipples one by one, smiled when she twisted his hair in her hands, groaned when she stroked him through his jeans.

He moved lower, kissing her stomach, the place where she'd carried their child, running his tongue over her skin, lower and lower, sliding off her underwear so he could kiss and tongue between her legs.

She gasped, holding his head, telling him all he needed to know with her pleasure-glazed eyes. He lingered, lost in their uncomplicated passion, the high of making her feel as good as she made him, spreading her thighs so he could lick her until she was clawing at his shoulders and crying out his name.

Wound too tight to wait any longer, he removed the last of his clothes, grabbed a condom from his wallet and covered himself, his fingers trembling with repressed need.

'Why did we wait so long?' she whispered as

his body covered hers, their legs entwined, hands roaming feverishly.

He gazed into the depth of her eyes. 'I have no idea.'

Holding her in his arms felt so right. Their passion seemed second nature. Their trust mutual after everything else they'd shared.

But he couldn't wait any longer. He covered her body with his, kissing her deep. She clung to him, her hands around his neck, her legs encircling his hips, her kisses growing frantic. 'Roman…'

His name was a plea on her lips and he finally relented, giving them what they both craved, pushing slowly inside her and then holding still but for the crazy beating of his heart.

'Are you okay?' he asked, panting, using every scrap of his willpower not to move.

'Yes. Don't stop.' She shifted under him, restless, needy, and he scrunched his eyes closed, seeing flashes of light, so intense was the pleasure.

He kissed her, swallowing up her mewls and moans as he gently thrust inside her, revelling in her hard-won trust and their strong emotional bond, which intensified his desire.

This time was so much better. He knew this woman. Her smile raised his spirits. Her sense of humour left him light-hearted. Her passion matched his, consuming him until she was all he could think about.

'Sadie…' he groaned as they held each other tight, the tempo building, each of them chasing the finish line.

Her nails dug into his skin as she gripped him tight. He pulled back from kissing her, stared into her beautiful eyes, now glazed with arousal. Their stares locked.

Despite everything, his own reticence, the promises he'd made, Sadie's warnings, something inside him reached out to her. He had no idea if could ever again love, but the new hopeful part of him she'd awoken wanted things: this deep emotional connection, the passion that left him speechless, a relationship with a woman who understood him and asked nothing of him that he couldn't give.

Now, moving inside her, he'd never felt more convinced that he was ready to try and open himself up to a new relationship.

With Sadie.

When Sadie shattered, crying out his name, his own climax tingled at the base of his spine, as if her pleasure was inexorably linked with his own. He groaned, staring down at her, and for a few blissful and heady seconds anything seemed possible while they were together like this.

As if she felt it too, Sadie gripped his face, holding his eyes to hers.

All his needs and wants coalesced. He was a flesh and blood man, yes, but since meeting Sadie, he had dreams and aspirations, hopes for the future. A future that included this beautiful, caring woman.

His orgasm tore at him. He buried his face against her neck, dragging in her scent, holding her so tight, she felt a part of him.

Having fought this physical release for so long, Roman already wanted Sadie again. Their bond was addictive. Sadie was balm to his body and soul. One he wasn't sure he could do without.

They held each other, catching their breath, kissing, laughing, the release of a year's worth of tension euphoric.

'Please tell me you can stay the night.' Sadie sighed, curling her body against his, her head resting over his thumping heart.

Roman stroked his fingers through her hair. He wanted that. Except he also wanted more.

Having Sadie in his arms while their daughter slept peacefully in the other room made the gaping holes in his life more evident, their edges sharper, their depths vast lonely spaces. He wanted to plan with her, to figure out a way they could be a family, know if Sadie felt the same way about him.

Did she see a future for the two of them? Or was she still too scared to look?

'I can stay the night, if you think it won't confuse Milly.' His hand caressed her shoulder as he pressed his lips to her forehead. He couldn't stop touching her.

'She's not even three months old.' Sadie smiled up at him. 'She's not going to remember seeing you in the morning and even if she could, you're her father.'

'Good point.' He drew her face up to his and kissed her lips.

He was Milly's father. He needed to be there for his girl. And he wanted to be there for Sadie too. No one could replace Karolina and Miko in his heart. But just as he'd found a new and limitless source of love for his daughter, perhaps there could also be space for another relationship. With Sadie.

'I know you have doubts,' Sadie said, staring up at him, 'but I hope you know that you're a great father.'

He hummed non-committally. 'Right now, all I can think about is how to be everything I need to be. How to do everything in my power to ensure that our girl is safe and happy.'

'Our girl,' Sadie whispered. 'I like that.'

He gripped her tighter, worried that he'd never let her go. 'I understand your fears for the future.'

Sadie stiffened, but Roman continued, needing some concession that they would have this necessary conversation. 'But promise me we'll talk about a plan for sharing the parental responsibilities some time. I know you've been hurt in the past. But I never thought I'd have a second chance at a family, and I never want to let anyone down again.'

Sadie raised her head from his chest, from the thump of his heart. 'What do you mean? You don't blame yourself for the accident, do you? Because it wasn't your fault.'

'Intellectually, I know I wasn't responsible,' he said, stroking her back. 'I didn't cause the accident. But there's a part of me that feels like I let my family down because I wasn't driving that day. I'll never know if I might have been able to avoid the collision, if I'd been behind the wheel instead of at work.'

'I'm so sorry,' she said, pressing her lips to his, her kiss a perfect distraction from his pain. 'I promise we'll talk about a shared custody arrangement,' she said, her stare glittering with fear and uncertainty, 'if you promise me one thing in return.'

'Anything.' He nodded, resolved to tread so carefully, to give Sadie the reassurance she needed. He didn't want to hurt her. If he rushed her, she'd withdraw, so damaged was her trust.

But could he be everything *he* needed to be, could he keep Milly safe and happy and be the things Sadie needed also? Perhaps living day to day was the right plan.

'Promise you won't over-promise.' She blinked, her stare so vulnerable, he wished he could kiss away all her fears. 'This has all happened so quickly. And people change their minds. As you said, it's Milly's happiness that's most important.'

So she *was* still scared for the future. She didn't see them as a couple, only as parents with some depressing amicably shared custody situation. And she was right. He couldn't promise more. Yes, he hoped they might be able to build on this intense chemistry and have a relationship, but he wasn't ready to fully risk his heart until he knew he could always be there for Milly.

Because Sadie's caution made sense: if it all went wrong, he could lose everything.

'I promise,' he said, her hesitation inflaming his own fears that he could be what both Milly and Sadie needed.

Satisfied with his word, she straddled him, kissed him, luring him back to the one certainty between them: their desire.

Roman closed his eyes and surrendered to his physical hunger.

Sadie didn't want to get hurt again and he

didn't want to be the one to let her down. Nor did he want to fail Milly, the way he'd failed Miko.

But caution and sense were no substitute for the passion that made him feel alive. Could Sadie's craving for him match his for her? Could she ever trust him, or was that a foolish illusion?

Did she expect any connection between the two of them to fail, and what if she was right?

His last thought, before his head filled with only Sadie once more, was now that his heart was inexorably linked with his little girl, the one thing he couldn't do was mess up this second chance at a family or risk losing another person he loved.

CHAPTER TWELVE

So how was last night?

GRACE'S TEXT CAME through the minute Sadie left
the Tube station and emerged on the wintry street
a short walk from the hospital. Roman had left
at the crack of dawn and her sister had spent the
night at her boyfriend's place. There had been
no time for more than a few words as Sadie had
handed over a fractious Milly to her sister and
rushed to work, relief nipping at her heels.

What was there to say?

Her night with Roman had been wonderful.

After their promises to each other, they'd made
love again with the same desperation as the time
before, as if both aware that their moments together, just Roman and Sadie, were limited.

But of course they were.

No matter how hard she tried to live in the moment, to savour every one of his kisses, to lavish
in the way he made her feel cherished and store

the amazing things he'd said to memory, harsh and uncertain reality was about to intrude.

Because her feelings seemed to have a life of their own. What if she allowed them free rein, allowed her guard to fall, opened herself up to a committed relationship with Roman, and he decided that she wasn't what he wanted after all? What if he changed his mind?

Images of a possible future flashed in her head like scenes from a horror movie. If Roman and Sadie didn't work out, what would happen to Milly? Would their daughter lose her wonderful father, or would Sadie be forced to see Roman every time they handed over Milly, be reminded over and over that, while he cherished the child they'd made, for him, Sadie wasn't good enough?

Was having him for herself worth the risk of losing everything, including her peace of mind?

She was terrified by her bone-deep fears, and the last thing she'd wanted was to discuss Roman with her twin. Sadie might as well be made of glass, her every emotion on display to her perceptive sister.

Hoping a few well-placed emojis would appease Grace, she fired off a reply.

Good. He adores Milly, but then what's not to love?

And it was true. Roman loved their daughter.

That didn't mean he had feelings for Sadie. He was in love with Karolina. And even if he could one day develop feelings for Sadie, she would always be second best. Could she live with that knowledge, that feeling of soul-destroying inadequacy, again?

With Roman as comparison, she now wondered how she'd ever failed to see through her ex. Roman had been right. She deserved better.

But there was one man for whom any woman, including Sadie, would never be enough: Roman.

Besides, she still had to get through the Valentine's Day auction. She still had to fix him up on a date with another woman, and he still planned to leave for Ireland afterwards. And she'd promised to discuss the future of Milly's custody...

Fighting the nauseated roll of her stomach, Sadie walked swiftly across the hospital car park to the rear staff entrance. Desperate to work as a distraction, she removed her scarf and coat and headed upstairs to Sunshine Ward.

As she arrived on the ward, she'd barely had a chance to glance at the patients on her list when Roman appeared at her side, looking drop-dead gorgeous dressed in one of his immaculate suits.

Her heart galloped with longing, mocking every word of denial she'd just spouted in her head.

'You're here early,' Sadie said, desperate to

kiss him hello the way they'd kissed goodbye a few hours ago.

'I slept incredibly well, Dr Barnes. I feel... rejuvenated,' he said, replacing the ward tablet into the charging station on the desk. Apart from the knowing look in his eyes, his manner was all business.

Sadie breathed through her hot flush, her body recalling every second of pleasure they'd shared.

'I wanted to check on Josh's progress, before my clinic,' he continued, his voice the professional one he used at work.

Sadie nodded, the surge of excitement shunting her heart rate trickling away. What had she expected? That he'd march onto the ward this morning declaring not only his paternity of Milly but also that he couldn't live without Sadie?

That was the ridiculous kind of stunt Mark would pull. Roman was twice the man.

Of course he wasn't on the ward to see her.

'And I've just admitted a six-year-old with a fractured clavicle and abdominal contusion following a road collision,' he continued, indicating the bay he'd come from. Roman's expression turned stony, so Sadie immediately knew that, of course, he was thinking of his family, of Karolina and Miko.

Sadie paused, desperate to reach out to him, missing the way that same voice had whispered her name as he'd moved inside her. 'Are you okay?'

But they weren't a couple.

Only, like Josh the presentation of this new patient was a little close to home for Roman.

He nodded, brushing aside her concern, so Sadie deflated. 'There's a small haematoma around the liver consistent with a seat-belt injury, but no signs of ongoing haemorrhage. I've prescribed IV analgesia, which the nurses are administering at the moment.'

Recalling how, last night, he'd confessed his fears that he'd let his family down, Sadie welcomed the reminder that Roman was still grieving for his wife and son. That no matter how close they'd seemed last night, he was still alone by choice.

It wasn't usual for consultants to perform everyday tasks, admitting patients and prescribing. But Roman liked to work, his self-prescribed antidote to his grieving process.

'Thank you,' she muttered, busying herself with some routine paperwork, disappointment twisting her insides.

While she'd spent last night agonising over every touch, every kiss and whisper, wondering if he might one day, if she waited around long enough, be ready for a relationship, Roman was still content to be the same workaholic loner planning to locum his way through his life. He couldn't help but love Milly, but that didn't mean he wanted Sadie.

As if proving her point, he lowered his voice. 'How's our girl this morning?'

Shoving aside depressing images of future Roman dropping in to see their daughter in between locum positions, or sending for her when she was old enough to travel overseas, Sadie forced her eyes to his. 'She's fine, a little bit grizzly. I think she's teething.'

She kept her voice low not to be overheard. As far as everyone at work knew, Roman was just the hottie surgeon with whom they could win a date.

'I've been thinking,' he said in the same quiet conspiratorial voice. 'I think you're right about the auction. Is it too late to pull out? I might have a friend who'll stand in for me.'

Sadie swallowed, her throat aching. He couldn't face dating anyone. He wasn't ready to put himself out there, not even for a good cause.

She was a fool to think he might one day be ready for more with her.

'I'm sure it will be fine,' she said, her vague hopes withering. 'I'll talk to Sammy.'

But of course he couldn't go through with the charade when he was still grieving for his wife, still in love with her, still dreading Valentine's Day.

'Is everything okay?' he asked, eyeing her with wariness that told her they were once more out of sync.

They might have been discussing a case or the cold snap in the weather for all the warmth between them.

'Fine. It's going to be a busy day, that's all.'

There was no chance of privacy and they each had jobs to do. He was on call that night and Sadie couldn't wait to get home to Milly, to cuddle away all her doubts.

Just then, the emergency alarm sounded.

A flurry of panicked activity surrounded the bedside of the boy Roman had just admitted.

Sadie rushed over, Roman following.

The little boy was struggling to catch a breath, his chest wheezing and his skin almost translucently pale and covered with a fine sheen of perspiration.

'He just went off,' his nurse explained. 'I'd just started the analgesia and was taking his observations when he stopped responding.'

While a concerned Roman placed an oxygen mask over his face, Sadie checked the boy's responsiveness and took his pulse, which was a weak and rapid flutter.

'Have we got a blood-pressure reading?'

Roman asked, glancing at Sadie, his stare almost frantic.

'Hypotensive. Eighty-five over fifty,' the nurse said.

'Could be anaphylaxis,' Sadie said, reaching for the IV to switch off the drip that was administering the painkiller that Roman had prescribed earlier that morning.

She shot him a reassuring look; she knew him so well now, understood how he would blame himself.

But he was focussed on the patient.

He turned to Sammy, who'd also arrived, wheeling in the emergency crash trolley. 'Can we have intramuscular adrenaline now, please?' Roman said, nodding to Sadie to insert a second IV cannula.

'Get rid of that drip and start some intravenous saline,' he ordered, his voice strained with self-reproach.

'Any documented allergies?' Sadie asked, both Roman and the boy's nurse shaking their heads.

Because she knew him so well, Sadie saw the guilt in Roman's expression.

An allergic reaction to a drug could be life-threatening.

But it wasn't his fault. Hopefully, there would be time to comfort him in private later.

'Call the next of kin, please,' Sadie instructed the nurse.

The nurse ducked out of the bay to call the boy's parents.

Instead of leaving Sadie to manage the emergency, as other busy consultants might do, Roman stayed, administering the adrenaline, jabbing the needle into the boy's leg muscles.

Sadie winced as the boy cried, but being responsive to pain in a shock situation was a good indicator that they'd treated the anaphylaxis in time.

'Saturations are ninety-three per cent.' Sadie met Roman's stare, trying to offer him reassurance.

For now the emergency was contained. Stopping the offending drug infusion had been the first treatment, and hopefully the adrenaline would work quickly to dampen the body's violent immune response to a foreign agent.

They faced each other for a few tense seconds, waiting, silently communicating their concerns in their stares.

Within seconds of the adrenaline injection being administered, the wheezing eased and the boy's colour improved. His heart rate slowed to a hundred and twenty beats per minute and his blood pressure rose.

Sadie shot Roman a hesitant smile. Despite

the uncertainties for the future, she and Roman were still a team when it mattered.

Everyone around the bed relaxed a fraction.

'It's okay, Tom.' Roman spoke to the frightened and tearful boy, resting his hand on Tom's shoulder. 'Your body didn't like the medicine we gave it but you're going to be okay. I'm sorry that I had to give you that nasty injection in the leg, but Mummy and Daddy are on their way to give you a hug.'

While Sammy and Tom's nurse soothed the boy, Roman and Sadie spoke away from the bedside.

'I'll keep an eye on him,' Sadie said, wanting more than anything to touch Roman and soothe those worry lines from around his eyes. But he still wasn't hers to comfort.

'Thank you,' he said, distracted, a helpless look haunting his eyes. 'I asked about allergies,' he muttered as if to himself. 'I checked with his mother.'

'Of course you did.' Sadie stared up at him, willing him to be gentle with himself. 'A case of an undocumented allergy could happen to anyone.'

Roman glanced back at Tom, concern still etched over his face.

Of course, if he lived with the guilt that he might have been able to help his beloved wife and cherished son if only he'd been with them that day, a caring doctor like Roman would sometimes struggle to stay impartial and not be triggered by the cases he saw.

Roman's pager sounded and he winced. 'That's clinic. I need to go.' He shot her a preoccupied smile that didn't quite reach his eyes. 'It's going to be one of those days. You're sure you're okay here?'

'Of course.' Sadie pasted on that brave face. 'I'll text you an update on Tom's progress.'

As he walked away Sadie sagged in defeat.

Their work was often demanding. But today, rather than pull together, they seemed to be drifting apart. How were they expected to discuss the big issues, like the custody of their daughter, when they seemed so distant once more?

Roman wasn't obligated to share his deepest fears with her, but it was obvious that, no matter what they'd shared, his family were clearly never far from his mind.

She'd always known it, but some secret part of her had hoped that their relationship might help him come to terms with his loss.

As she set about her morning duties, a busy morning making the night before, the closeness she'd imagined, feel like a distant dream, she clung to the timely reminder that the only part of Roman available was the part she'd had from the start.

They'd enjoyed one more night together before reality dawned, but she wouldn't torture herself with doubt-fuelled maybes. She needed to start weaning herself off, to check the lock on her heart and move forward, putting their baby first.

Because no matter what the future held, she wouldn't be second best again. Not even for Roman.

CHAPTER THIRTEEN

IN THE EARLY hours of the following morning, Roman swished opened the bedside curtains of his newest patient—a thirteen-year-old boy with suspected torsion of the testis—and headed for the nearest computer terminal to order an urgent ultrasound scan.

Accident and Emergency was surprisingly quiet. There were no urgent, on-call surgeries requiring his attention, but Roman knew he wouldn't be able to sleep a wink. Better to keep busy with work than to toss and turn the night away thinking around and around in circles about his situation with Sadie.

Not that she was very far from his thoughts no matter how he tried to occupy his mind. Today they had seemed to go two steps back in their emotional journey. She'd been evasive on the ward earlier, when all he'd wanted to do was get her alone and tell her about the plans brewing in his head, plans she probably wasn't ready to hear.

Roman pressed send on the scan request and sighed.

Every time he and Sadie inched closer to some sort of discussion of the future that might settle the worst of his anxieties for Milly's well-being, Sadie backed off. She wasn't keen on the idea of Milly visiting Prague. She hadn't told anyone that he was Milly's father. She wasn't even interested that, because of his feelings for Sadie, he felt increasingly uncomfortable about going ahead with the auction.

When it came to their relationship and future for them as a family, she was like a wisp of smoke, vague and elusive, slipping further through his fingers.

How could he confess all of his ideas and dreams and hopes, when each sliver of her trust gained cost him the slamming-up of another of her barriers? How could he broach the subject of them having a proper relationship, when she wasn't even curious about his plans to leave London? He understood her fear. He was scared too. But as long as they trusted each other, they could make anything work...

Except not knowing how Sadie felt was driving him crazy. Perhaps he'd given her enough time...

He was just about to select the next surgical patient waiting to be seen when he saw Sadie rush into the ED clutching a wrapped-up Milly in her arms.

His blood ran cold.

His body lurched in their direction, feet skidding to a halt inside the resus room where they'd been ushered by a nurse.

'What's wrong?' he said, concern for his daughter trumping social niceties.

Milly was flushed and fractious, restless in Sadie's arms.

'She's fine.' Sadie shot him a reassuring look, but he saw her worry.

Roman dismissed Sadie's assurance, his eyes scouring the baby for signs of what was wrong. 'If she's *fine*, you wouldn't have brought her to hospital in the middle of the night.'

'I thought she was teething,' Sadie said, taking a seat and undressing Milly on her lap so one of the ED doctors—a young guy who appeared to be barely out of medical school—could examine a grizzling Milly.

'But Grace said she's had a cold today, sniffling, a mild temperature. Nothing alarming,' Sadie explained to the young doctor as if she was completely unaware of the panic building inside Roman's chest.

Roman moved to stand at Sadie's side, his hand resting on her shoulder for comfort, although he couldn't be certain which of them needed it more.

'She spiked a fever tonight at bedtime,' Sadie continued and Roman winced, wishing she'd called him, 'and wouldn't settle with paracetamol. I tried sponging her down with tepid water, but her temperature stayed high.'

He felt Sadie stiffen and steeled himself. 'She had a convulsion about thirty minutes ago.'

Every bone in Roman's body threatened to collapse. His hands itched to reach for his darling Milly, who was alert but grumbling pitifully, the sound designed to tug at his heart and urge him into action to protect his daughter.

'Has she had a seizure before?' the junior doctor asked, glancing at Roman and taking in the surgical scrubs and his hospital security tag.

'No,' Sadie and Roman said together. Roman checked Milly's bare torso and limbs, noting the absence of a rash.

Because the ED doctor was now frowning at Roman, trying to figure out his role, Roman educated him.

'I'm Milly's father,' he said, loud enough for his voice to carry so the entire ED might hear. 'I'm a consultant paediatric surgeon at this hospital, and her mother works here as a paediatric registrar.'

How could Sadie be so calm? Why wasn't she barking orders and ordering tests?

The guy nodded and returned his attention to

Milly, performing an examination of her neurological system.

Sadie glanced at Roman, her stare accusing, as if he was losing it. Well, newsflash, he was close. This was his baby in distress. She'd had a seizure.

'How long did the seizure last?' the doctor asked.

'Not more than a minute,' Sadie said, apologetically, while he tried to examine a crying Milly while her doctor parents looked on.

But Roman didn't care about treading on toes when it came to his daughter's safety. He and Sadie were senior specialists. They had more combined experience than this youngster. He was moments away from snatching Milly up and assessing her himself.

As if she sensed his restlessness, Sadie rested her hand on his and continued giving a history. 'It appeared to be a generalised seizure, with symmetrical tonic-clonic jerking of her limbs and momentary loss of consciousness.'

Roman winced, berating himself for not being there. How could he have been so…preoccupied with his feelings for Sadie when there were more important things to worry about? How could he have let Milly down when he'd made her a promise in his heart? How would he survive if anything terrible happened…?

'Post-ictal drowsiness lasted five minutes,'

Sadie said, flicking a cautious glance at Roman, as if she could tell he was worried sick, 'but she was rousable throughout.'

Because he was so far beyond worry, Roman's frantic mind helpfully provided a list of worst-case scenarios, serious life-threatening infections that might be responsible for Milly's temperature, most of which he couldn't bear to contemplate. But his medical training wouldn't allow him to wallow in ignorance.

Febrile convulsions were common in infants and young children. This one, Milly's first, sounded simple in nature. As long as there was no recurrence in the next twenty-four hours, the prognosis for this being an isolated event was good.

But this was *his* daughter. He wanted every test ordered, every serious infection ruled out. Every consultant in the hospital awoken to come and tend to his sick little girl.

'Any history of epilepsy in the family?' The doctor looked at both Roman and Sadie, who shook their heads.

'And no history of head trauma?' he asked.

'No,' Sadie confirmed.

Roman paced while the guy, to his credit, performed a thorough examination, including looking inside Milly's ears. No mean feat given that she was now wailing and writhing in Sadie's lap.

The minute he'd finished, Roman took the baby and rocked her gently. She was flushed and cross, hot to the touch, her temperature still reading thirty-nine degrees.

'I think you should order some tests,' Roman said. 'A lumbar puncture is indicated in an infant under six months of age with a first seizure.'

As if she wanted to distance herself from Milly's neurotic father, Sadie said nothing, eyeing him warily. But Roman knew the statistics. Despite the lack of clinical signs—neck stiffness, photophobia, a rash—they needed to exclude meningitis as a cause of Milly's fever.

'I... I...' the young doctor stuttered, his stare darting between Roman and Sadie.

'Roman...' Sadie rose and stood at his side, cooing to Milly and slipping her arm around his waist. 'Let him do his job.'

He stared, pleading through every pore of his body. Couldn't she feel the tension in him, the fear and explosive impotence building inside him like contained steam that brought to mind every horrific outcome of a missed diagnosis?

He couldn't lose his daughter.

'We will perform a lumbar puncture,' the doctor said, his voice impressively calm, to his credit standing up to Roman's unyielding authority. 'But she also has a middle ear infection on the left, which as you know is enough to trigger a febrile convulsion. The eardrum has actually perforated, which will ease the pain that was most likely the cause of her being difficult to settle tonight.'

Roman breathed for the first time since Sadie and Milly had walked into the ED, but it was still only ten per cent of his usual lung capacity.

'With your consent,' the doctor continued, addressing them both, 'I'll start Milly on some antibiotics, which should help to tackle the fever.'

'Thank you,' Sadie said, while Roman pressed his lips to Milly's soft and downy head, shushing her gently while he tried to rein in the urge to wake the entire hospital.

Within minutes, they were moved from Resus to a regular bay with a stretcher and two hard plastic chairs. Sadie sat and tried to nurse Milly, who drank intermittently, clearly wanting the comfort of her mother's breast, but also lacking much of an appetite.

Still wound tight, Roman paced the small space, coming to a halt when a nurse appeared with a syringe of pink liquid that she gently squeezed into Milly's mouth.

Milly cried and fussed for endless minutes as if she couldn't get comfortable. Roman silently prayed for his daughter's relief, vowing never again to minimise the concerns of his patients' parents.

As he looked at Milly, another promise solidified. No matter the status of his and Sadie's relationship, he would be there for Milly, every day of her life. He'd fight her corner while she was too young to do it for herself and dry her tears. Even if it killed him, he'd be the father she deserved.

Everything else, even his feelings, paled into insignificance.

'Don't you need to get back to work?' Sadie asked eventually once Milly had fallen into a restless sleep.

'No. I'm a consultant,' Roman said, fighting the urge to wrap his daughter up in cotton wool from head to toe. 'My registrar is here somewhere.' He waved his hand dismissively, wondering anew at Sadie's appearance of calm.

Wearing just a nappy, his tiny daughter was curled up on the soft white sheet, her skin almost translucently pale.

He couldn't even adjust the blanket to cover her given they were trying to bring down her fever. How would he protect her from the world, from the scraped knees and the mean words in the playground? From disappointment and heartache?

'I think they should admit her for tests,' he added, helplessness still crawling over his skin like nettle rash.

Sadie looked at him as if he'd grown a second head, but her voice was soft when she spoke. 'It's only an ear infection. There's no need to over-react.'

'Overreact…?' Couldn't she tell how he clung to his fear, his terror, with all his might? If he freed everything he was feeling inside for all to see, she would understand his current levels of restraint.

'How can you be so calm?' he asked, jealous now of Sadie's ability to live in the moment and not plot out every worst-case scenario like a mind map of doom.

'Please sit down,' she said, her voice tinged with sympathy, her stare soft.

But could she truly see the depth of his fear for Milly? Did she know him well enough after everything they'd been through to understand how tonight had, not only triggered his grief over Miko, but also inflamed his insecurities that he could ever be a good enough father to keep his baby safe?

Because every second that he delayed the big discussion he and Sadie needed to have was a second where he wasn't fully a part of his daughter's life.

And he needed to be.

'I'm worried too,' Sadie said, taking his hand again when he folded himself stiffly into the spare chair. 'And I understand where your mind is going.'

He swallowed. He couldn't lose another person he loved. It would destroy him.

He'd never wanted to be this vulnerable again, but darling Milly had found a way to come into their lives, and from the second he'd known her he'd been powerless against the flood of paternal love that had swept him off his feet.

'But look—she's quiet now, sleeping like a baby,' Sadie said, in her soothing doctor's voice, because Roman had opened up to her, exposed his grief, shown her his broken pieces.

She wrapped her arms around him and held him tight. 'I brought her in to be checked over, but we both know that febrile convulsions affect one in twenty children. The chances of another seizure fall as her temperature drops. And hopefully this will never happen again.'

When she eased back to observe him, Roman scrubbed a hand over his face, feeling a hundred years old. 'You're right. But she's not leaving here until she's seen the paediatric team on call. You and I are too close to be objective. I want an impartial expert opinion.'

Sadie nodded. 'I agree.'

They fell into a tense silence, holding hands while they watched their daughter breathe in and breathe out.

For Roman, there was no longer any debate. He needed to live near his daughter. Regardless of their romantic aspirations, he and Sadie were Milly's parents, the three of them a family.

They always would be.

But the time had come to discuss the future because, more than anything else, he unapologetically needed to keep his loved ones safe.

CHAPTER FOURTEEN

To Roman's relief, by the time Milly's lab results were back, the all-clear from the point of view of a more serious infection, she was almost back to her smiling, gurgling self. But while he'd watched her sleep fitfully, pacing her room while Sadie dozed in the chair, he'd come to some big decisions.

'I'm taking some sick days to stay home with her,' Roman said while they waited for the discharge papers to be signed. He couldn't wait to have Milly out of the hospital, as if just by being there she was at risk of a relapse.

'There's no need,' Sadie said, once more eyeing him as if he'd grown a second head. 'I have the next two days off. I'll be home with her.'

'I want to be there.' He cuddled Milly close, whispering Czech endearments, while he fought for the threads of his composure. 'I'm her father.'

'I know that,' she said, her voice tinged with

resentment. 'The whole hospital knows now after your announcement in the ED last night.'

Roman winced, remorse a hot rush through his veins. 'I'm genuinely sorry if that upset you, but I'm proud that this beautiful baby is mine. Last night was terrifying. It made me realise a few things.'

He'd given Sadie as much time as he could to come to terms with the fact that he was going to be a permanent fixture in Milly's life. The minute she'd told him that they'd made a baby together, he'd been brainstorming possible solutions, knowing that there was really only one answer that worked: him living where Milly lived.

Where Sadie lived, too. Because he had feelings for her. Feelings that he wanted to explore as they continued their relationship. Feelings he'd only ever had for one other woman.

Time for them to talk.

Sadie stood, holding her arms out for the baby. 'I was scared, too. But the worst-case scenario didn't happen.' She took a deep breath, clearly searching for patience. 'Let's just both go home, have a shower, try to get some sleep. Everything will sort itself out.'

Frustration gripped him; he needed to make her understand his point of view, because if he didn't do something definitive to safeguard his family, fear would tear him apart.

'I know you don't want to discuss it, Sadie, but I had a lot of time to think last night, and the moment has come for us to face facts.'

Fear clouded Sadie's tired eyes. 'What facts do you mean?'

They were both exhausted. Except as he'd watched the sun dawn over London from Milly's hospital room, he'd found the clarity that had eluded him since Sadie had come back into his life.

He no longer wanted the lonely life he'd tolerated before. He needed to find a way to make them work as a family. And he wanted him and Sadie to try and have a relationship. Except voicing all of that would scare her away.

Roman hesitated, reached for Sadie's hand. 'I'll be honest, when you first told me about Milly, I was terrified that I wouldn't be able to love her the way I should as her father. I spent so long shutting myself down, you see.'

Sadie nodded, her eyes glistening with emotion.

'But loving Milly happened so naturally,' he continued, his voice tight, 'and it helped me to remember more of the happy everyday moments I had with Miko.'

Sadie stared in silence so he carried on. 'Last night, while I watched our girl sleep, everything became crystal-clear. I need to live where she lives. It's the only option that makes sense. The only option I can tolerate. I'm moving to London.'

Holding Milly like a shield, Sadie paced across the room. 'We said we'd take it one day at a time. You can't just drop that bombshell and expect me to agree. You're being irrational, making big decisions when you're clearly emotional after yesterday...'

Roman tensed, his body chilled with apprehension. 'I thought you'd be happy. I'm not breaking my promise to you. We will take one day at a time, but we can do it together, not apart.'

'We can't discuss this now,' she said, dismissively, as if she'd never once given the future for them a thought.

Unlike that night at her place when they'd seemed to be on the same page emotionally and physically, when the possibility of a relationship had been a tangible thing, now he had no idea what Sadie wanted. But it was clear she continued to think only a few days ahead.

'Milly is sick,' she continued making excuses, 'and we have the fundraiser to get through and then you'll be leaving for Ireland. We can talk about everything else when you get back.'

'I don't care about the fundraiser. I told you I'll find someone else to take my place.' Nothing mattered but the three of them building on what they'd found. The three of them being together as a family.

Why couldn't she see that?

She looked down, pale and sombre. 'You're right; you shouldn't feel forced to date someone when you're not ready. I'll talk to Sammy, explain that you felt coerced, that because of your past, what you've been through, you were always going to be the wrong person…'

She thought he wanted to pull out because he was still in love with Karolina. He would always love his wife, but she wasn't the only reason he couldn't stomach the Valentine's charade. The main reason was Sadie.

Except where he was laying himself bare, she was still holding back, keeping her emotions safe, showing him that she trusted him with their daughter but not with her own heart.

Was she really so blind to his feelings? Had he alone experienced their growing closeness, so powerful that being intimate with her again had robbed him of breath?

Perhaps she was just scared that things were moving too fast.

'Sadie.' He stepped close and cupped her face, willing her to see him, to listen while he opened up deeply buried wounded parts of himself that he'd never expected to again see the light of day. 'I don't care about the auction because I don't want to date another woman, even for a good cause. I only want to date you.'

She gasped, a spark of the passion he'd been hoping to see flaring bright in her eyes.

'Tell me I'm not alone in wanting that? Be honest,' he continued, his throat raw with everything he left unsaid. 'Tell me what *you* want.'

She turned her face away but not before he saw a flash of longing in her expression. 'I'm not sure what I want is relevant. I'm a mother. I have to put Milly first.'

'What does that mean?' Fear twisted his gut. That was exactly what he was trying to do: put Milly first. That didn't mean he couldn't also pursue a relationship with Sadie. But was that relationship one-sided? Was Sadie still living in the moment that she clung to so ferociously, still classifying them as a casual fling, something she expected to fizzle out any day now?

'It means that whatever is going on with us is meaningless compared to what we want for our daughter.'

She looked up, meeting his stare, acting as if they'd made the same argument, but from Roman's point of view they were speaking a different language. Right from day one she'd expected nothing from their connection, and not even these past couple of incredible weeks, working together, spending time as a family, making love and opening up to each other, had changed her view.

To Sadie, Roman was doomed to let her down, the one thing he vowed never to do. She expected them to fail. She saw no future for the two of them beyond their roles as parents, because she still didn't trust him enough. She wasn't even willing to give them a try.

'So everything we've been through together,' he said, 'everything we've shared, was meaningless to you?'

Had he allowed himself to get carried away in their relationship? Maybe because a part of his heart would always be broken, the part that beat for Karolina, he'd failed to inspire Sadie's absolute trust.

Maybe it was his fault that they were so emotionally discordant because she believed he couldn't be the man she needed.

But he was at least willing to try.

She flushed with shame. 'I'm not saying that. I just don't think we should be making any life-changing decisions right now.'

'I disagree,' he said with all the passion he felt for this woman. 'We only get one life and I don't want to waste another second of mine being away from Milly when I could be there for her, a proper father to the best of my abilities.'

Tears filled Sadie's eyes as she stared. 'You

are her father. I'd never stand in the way of your relationship.'

The unspoken *but* echoed around the room.

'Okay, well, if you won't tell me what you want, I'll put myself out there first: I want you, too, Sadie. I want us to try and have a proper relationship. I'm happy to go at your pace, because I understand you're scared to be hurt, but I want you to trust me. I want us to be a family. You, me and Milly.'

Pain twisted her features as tears slid down her cheeks. 'I do trust you…' she said in a broken whisper. 'But if you want my honest answer, tell me one thing first. Before Karolina and Miko died, did you want more children?'

Roman frowned, jolted by the shift of topic. Then he realised where this was going. Despite creating their beautiful daughter, Sadie still saw herself as somehow defective because of her fertility problems and the way she'd been let down by her ex.

'Yes. We talked about it,' he said, defeated, wanting to be transparent even though the truth would hurt her. 'In fact, we were trying for another child when she was killed.'

Sadie's face paled. She nodded, as if he'd handed her the winning argument on a plate. 'Thank you for being honest.'

He rushed to her, took her in his arms, kissed

her forehead and whispered, 'I'm sorry to hurt you. But I want to be honest. We've always had that, haven't we? But I'm a different man now from the one I was with Karolina.'

He could never be the same after what had happened to his family, but that didn't make him and his feelings for Sadie any less. 'I'm ready to try again,' he continued. 'With you, if you want the same thing.'

She sniffed, slipping on a brave mask as she looked up at him with resolve. 'It's okay for you to want something that isn't me, Roman. You come from a big family, you wanted more children and you deserve to be happy. But I promised myself that I would never accept second place again. And for a man who already loves another woman, a man who dreams of another child, I'm a bad risk.'

'I don't care about having more children.' He gripped her shoulders, willing her to hear his truth. 'What matters is that I treasure Milly, take nothing for granted and never let her down.'

'I agree,' Sadie said, now eerily calm. 'That's what I've been trying to tell you. We both need to be there for our daughter and if we don't focus our attention there, we could mess that up for her.'

'But what about what we want for ourselves?'

he whispered, losing his grip on Sadie. Or perhaps he'd never had her in the first place.

Her eyes shone with tears. 'I stopped asking myself what I wanted in my twenties, when I had my infertility diagnosis. What I want—' she rested her hand on his chest '—doesn't matter, because I can't ever be what *you* need.'

Her fingers curled into his scrub top as if she might hold on and never let go. 'Milly was my miracle, Roman, but I can't give you more children. You say it doesn't matter now, but it might come to matter. It might matter very much one day.'

'I'm not that man, Sadie. I won't let you down.'

She shook her head, dismissing his promise. 'I know you'd never intentionally hurt me. But you've already been through so much loss. I couldn't bear to be the reason for your heartache if one day you decided you wanted another child more than you wanted me. Nor could I survive one day seeing in your eyes that I wasn't quite good enough. Can you blame me for holding something back to protect myself from that knowledge?'

Roman opened his mouth to argue, his jaw slack.

His stomach lurched with the familiar taste of defeat. After everything they'd been through, after everything they'd shared, she was choosing to protect herself from rejection that might never come, where he was exposing his battered and bruised heart and handing it to her on a platter.

She trusted him, but not enough.

'So that's it?' he asked, hoping with all his heart that she'd relent, that she'd throw her arms around his neck and trust her heart in his hands. 'That's all you're willing to risk?'

She tilted her chin, determined. 'Yes. Now I'm taking Milly home. When you return from Ireland, we can talk again, figure out a way to parent Milly together, but I think it's best if we put her first.'

Defeated, Roman nodded and stepped back. This was all she was willing to give. If he pushed her for more, he might lose everything: Sadie, what little trust they'd built up to now and, most devastating, Milly.

As if Sadie's fear were contagious, it gripped his throat, choking him. As choices went, he had no choice. He'd been there once before, so he knew with absolute certainty that he wouldn't survive losing another person he loved.

CHAPTER FIFTEEN

*Dr Roman Ježek, consultant paediatric
surgeon from Prague...*

WAS A WONDERFUL MAN, lover and father, and
she'd thrown him away...

Disgusted, Sadie deleted her sixth attempt to
write Roman's bio for the Valentine's Day auction that night, her finger stabbing angrily at the
delete key. But the only person she had to be
angry with was herself.

Taking her eyes off the accusing blank page
before her, Sadie glanced over the top of her laptop to where Grace was playing with Milly, her
heart a tender ache in her chest. Grace wheeled
the wooden duck toy from Roman through
Milly's line of vision. The baby, now fully recovered from the ear infection that had led to
Sadie's soul-destroying showdown with Roman,
squealed with excitement.

Sadie sighed, fixated on Roman's simple gift

and what it had represented. Their first outing together as a family, a day of blossoming love between father and daughter, hope for the future.

Of course, that unbreakable bond still stretched ahead of Milly and Roman. Sadie had no doubt that they would always have a wonderful relationship, be a close family. Roman wouldn't let Milly down.

But that bright future awaiting Roman and Milly wouldn't include Sadie. She'd messed up, thrown his dreams for the three of them as a family back in his face, breaking her own heart in the process.

No wonder she couldn't compose a single word.

'Shouldn't you be working on his bio instead of watching Milly's tummy time?' Grace said, scooping Milly into her lap so the baby too faced Sadie, as if with accusation.

Sadie rested her head in her hand. The trouble was, every time she tried to summarise Roman Ježek into an appealing few lines of type, his handsome face swam before her eyes on the screen. All the wonderful things he'd said at the hospital that day returning to haunt her.

He wanted to date her. He wanted them to try and have a relationship. He wanted the three of them to be a family.

Sadie stared with stinging eyes, not bothering to plead ignorance about who *he* was. She'd never been able to hide anything from Grace. It was a twin thing.

'Why don't you just ask him for his CV? That would be a start at least,' Grace said, spinning the cheerful yellow wheels of the pull-along duck.

Although Sadie hadn't seen Roman since that terrible day, she'd spoken to him every evening on the phone. Grace didn't know about the fat silent tears of anguish that had fallen down Sadie's face for the entire duration of last night's three-minute phone call, where they'd talked about Milly's improving health, her impending childhood immunisations, about the fact that she seemed to be teething.

But not about them. Because there was no them.

Roman had accepted that Sadie had given all she could give, and she'd run scared, pushing away his wonderful offer. After what he'd been through, it had been easy to convince him that it was best to focus on being parents together, that neither of them could risk losing what they had, the way she'd convinced herself.

Except she'd spent every hour since certain that, by taking the safest option, she'd made the biggest mistake of her life.

'Why don't you just write that you're cancelling his auction because you're in love with him?'

Grace said, standing and ambling over to Sadie with Milly in her arms.

Rather than deny the accusation, Sadie bit her lip to contain the crushing pain in her chest.

'Sometimes love isn't enough,' Sadie said, reaching for the baby for comfort.

Of course she loved Roman. Desperately. Now that she'd sabotaged their relationship, it was clear. How could she not fall for such an amazing man? But just like her wants, her love, too, was irrelevant.

'It's enough that he's committed to Milly,' she continued as Grace plopped down on the nearby sofa. 'He adores her. I can't let anything get in the way of that.'

Only, Roman wasn't the kind of man to act or speak rashly. Yes, he'd been scared for Milly. That didn't mean his declarations weren't well considered and genuine. It must have been agonising for him, after everything he'd been through, to bravely put himself out there and fight for her and Milly, for the three of them as a family. Especially when Sadie had clung to her fear that she wasn't good enough for Roman, that he loved Milly, but could never love Sadie.

'Including the fact that he might love you too?' Grace didn't believe in sugar coating.

Sadie shook her head, refusing to consider the

possibility. 'He loves Milly. He wants us to be a sort of family. But he doesn't love me.'

Roman loved Karolina and Miko and Milly. His devotion to their daughter was enough for Sadie.

'He's been through so much, he deserves happiness,' she continued, cuddling Milly close for comfort. 'What if he wants more children and I can't give them to him…?'

Except what if Roman did have strong feelings for her? What if that was enough? What if she'd allowed fear to overwhelm her just because Mark had made her feel inadequate over her fertility issues? Wasn't having any part of Roman better than having no part at all?

'You hate *what ifs*,' Grace pointed out.

Nauseated, Sadie closed the laptop. She should have given Roman a chance instead of shutting him down. She should have embraced what *she* wanted and gone after it. She should have kept her promise and discussed the future. So what if it was uncertain? Wasn't that its very definition? If Roman didn't care about having more children, Sadie should believe her own hype to live in the moment and trust his word.

Was it too late?

'You're right, I do.' Excitement pounded through her veins. She should tell Roman how she felt about him and just take one day at a time.

To hope that they could make a relationship work and, one day, he might love her the way she loved him. The opposite, embracing her fear, seeing him all the time because of Milly, never knowing how her future might have looked different if only she'd been honest and brave, didn't bear thinking about.

Handing Milly back to Grace, Sadie headed for the shower. 'I need to get ready for the fundraiser.'

'You haven't finished his bio,' Grace called, playing peekaboo with Milly from behind a cushion.

'I'll make something up.'

She knew all the important things about Roman by heart. She knew he was the best man she'd ever met. She knew his heartfelt declarations meant more than a million flashy red roses. She knew, as he'd tried to promise, that he'd never intentionally let her down. And she knew the depth of her love for him.

As she stepped under the spray of water, she closed her eyes, praying that what she knew would be enough.

Valentine's Day evening, Soho's Thames Gallery was decked out with tables and a stage for the much-anticipated hospital fundraiser, lights dimmed and atmosphere abuzz, most of the hospital staff and their families dolled up in black tie.

Roman waited in the shadows at one side of the stage, his stomach knotted with dread. He'd arrived late after collecting his Czech friend, Xaver, from the station. His old surgical colleague from Prague was now working in Oxford and had agreed to be auctioned in Roman's place. Roman had considered going through the motions himself, but his feelings for Sadie wouldn't allow it, even though they weren't reciprocated.

Now all he wanted to do was see Sadie. Maybe it wasn't too late to tell her how he felt. Maybe there was something to salvage. Maybe he'd given up too easily, lured off course by the argument of ensuring Milly's happiness.

But this wasn't about their daughter; it was about them, him and Sadie.

Braced for the agony ripping through his chest, Roman watched Sadie approach the microphone from the other side of the stage.

She looked stunning in a black gown with a beaded bodice, her hair sexily tousled, silver earrings sparkling in her ears. Roman curled his fingers into fists, fighting the urge to stride on stage and kiss her until she changed her mind about them and gave him a chance.

The background music stopped, and she gripped the microphone, nervously clearing her throat.

'Ladies and gentlemen. I hope you're all enjoying the evening.' She paused for the round of applause, her stare scanning the spacious room as if she was looking for Roman.

He'd texted her that he would be there, that he was working on a plan. He would wait until she announced him and then join her on stage with Xaver, declaring the last-minute substitution.

'The next auction,' she said, her voice tremulous, 'is the highlight you've all been waiting for: A date with an eligible doctor.'

The room erupted with cheers and whoops.

'I know you've all been looking forward to this one.' Sadie's smile turned feeble as she glanced down at the sheet of paper in her hand. 'But thing is, I've...um... I've messed up.'

Roman's heart thumped erratically. He ached to march on stage and wrap her in his arms, to tell her that she didn't need to go through with this, because he was in love with her. Except she didn't even want to discuss them having a relationship, let alone their feelings.

Sadie scrunched up the sheet of paper and glanced down at her feet. The audience fell silent, waiting.

Roman stepped forward, ready to show himself, to let her know that the auction could go ahead, but some instinct held him back.

Sadie raised her chin, addressing the crowd

with determination. 'You see, Dr Roman Ježek had kindly volunteered for this auction, but he's not here tonight.'

Before the groans of disappointment could drown her out, she rushed on. 'It's really not his fault. It's mine, but I've already said that... You see, I met Dr Ježek a year ago, funnily enough at another Valentine's Day event. And, well…we had a relationship. And a daughter, in fact. Milly, although that's by the by—'

She was rambling the way she did when she was nervous. Roman froze, his breath stalling. He wanted to hear where this was going.

'And anyway,' she continued, her hands twisting the paper, 'neither of us had been looking for a relationship and Dr Ježek signed up for this fundraiser in good faith, because he is a wonderful man and a brilliant doctor and an amazing father.'

She stopped abruptly, swallowing as if choked.

Unable to stand still a moment longer, Roman stepped forward, only to have his path blocked by the formidable Sister Samuels, who held out her arm like a barrier. He almost didn't recognise her out of uniform, she looked so glamorous. But he recognised her no-nonsense expression and stayed where he was.

'And the thing is,' Sadie said, her voice small, 'he wanted us to be a proper family, for me and him to have a real relationship, and I want that more than anything.'

She held her hand to her chest. 'But I got scared, you see, and I wouldn't listen to his dreams for the future when he tried to tell me about them. And now he's going to go to Ireland when I really want him to stay here, not just for Milly's sake, but for me. Because, the thing is...' she sighed '... I've fallen in love with him and I didn't tell him that, and now he's not here... And I might not get the chance now...'

She loved him?

Roman's heart climbed into his throat.

'But the final thing I wanted to say is this—' She faced the audience defiantly. 'Even if he were here tonight, this auction couldn't possibly go ahead. Because *I* want to date him. I want us to be a couple. I want us to be a family: me, him and Milly. And if he was here, that's what I'd say, so...'

Finally running out of steam, she glanced to the other organisers, who appeared either gobsmacked by the turn of events or on the verge of tears at Sadie's heartfelt speech.

Stunned, Roman itched to go to her. He needed to look into her eyes to see if what she'd said was true. He needed to tell her that he loved her too. That they'd work everything else out, together.

Sadie stood tall, gripping the mic and pasting

on a bright smile. 'We'll just move on to the next auction: a couples skydiving adventure.'

Without waiting for the crowd's reaction, Sadie hurried from the stage and Sammy dropped her arm.

Roman took off running.

CHAPTER SIXTEEN

CLOSE TO TEARS, Sadie left the stage, shaking her head at the other organisers as she hurried past. If she stopped to talk, she'd break down. She couldn't believe Roman hadn't shown up for his auction. Obviously she'd hurt him too much. Perhaps he'd already left for Ireland.

She'd missed her chance.

Biting back a sob of despair, Sadie left the backstage area as the auctions continued and exited the gallery into a dark staff corridor, the roar of pain in her head drowning out everything but her own words of recrimination.

He'd offered her a chance for them to be a family, offered her almost everything she wanted, and, instead of grabbing it with both hands, she'd succumbed to her cowardice and now she'd lost the man she loved.

Now that he was gone, she could see their relationship with alarming clarity. He'd shown her that he cared through his actions, he'd made her feel safe and cherished and desired. He'd been honest, and trustworthy and dependable, and she'd retreated, closed off, stayed safe.

Someone gripped her arm, spinning her around. Roman was there, dressed for the auction.

Sadie gasped, clutching her crumpled ball of paper to her chest. 'You made it?'

He looked gorgeous, the tux suiting his colouring, his blue eyes bright.

He gripped her upper arms, his thumbs gliding over her skin as if he couldn't bear to keep his hands to himself. 'Sorry I was late. I had to meet a friend at the station.'

He cupped her face, holding her stare captive. 'That was some grand declaration you just made. I thought you hated those?'

His eyes burned into hers, the intensity breathtaking.

Sadie gripped his arms, worried if she didn't hold onto him, he'd disappear. 'You heard that?'

He'd been there all along? Her brain couldn't compute why he was there, but her heart leaped at the sight of him.

He nodded, his smile indulgent. 'Every amazing word.'

She smiled, eyes stinging with unshed tears, her legs jelly. 'Well, I used to hate them, but then I met this man who showed me that sometimes you just have to be honest and say what you want. That some risks are worth taking.'

Before she could utter another word, Roman backed her up against the wall. Their eyes locked for a split second and then his lips descended, covering hers in a crushing kiss.

With euphoria spiking her blood, Sadie clung to his waist as she kissed him back. All of the pining and heartache of the past few days left her in a rush. He was there. If she held on tight, he'd have to stay.

When they parted for air, both panting, Roman rested his forehead against hers. 'Sorry. I sensed another one of your nervous rambles and I've missed kissing you.'

'Me too.' She rested her head on his chest, felt the pound of his heart against her cheek. 'I'm so sorry, Roman. I'm sorry that I pushed you away. I was scared. I doubted my instincts, because they'd steered me wrong in the past.' She looked up at him. 'But you helped me to see that the last time I'd tried to have a relationship, I'd still been grieving my diagnosis, grieving for that part of myself I assumed was out of reach. I ignored the warning signs that he wasn't the man for me because I was grateful that someone wanted me even though I was broken.'

Now was her chance to tell him that she loved him, that she'd been stupid, that she wanted any sort of relationship he was ready for. 'I meant what I said out there. I love you, and I'll take any part of you I can have. I know what I want now. I want you. I want us. I want the three of us to be a family.'

He stared, fiercely, his eyes darting over her face, as if he was scared to trust what she said. 'You really love me?' he asked, his expression tortured.

'Yes. How could I not? You're kind of wonderful. I think I fell in love with you when you opened the office door that time I was stuck. I was just too stupid to recognise my feelings.'

He kissed her again, pressing her against the wall.

This time when he pulled back, he appeared resolved. 'Sadie, it's time to talk about the future.'

Sadie nodded, raising her chin. 'I know, and I'm ready to lay myself open emotionally, to plan with you, to be the strong, unflinching woman you need.'

'Sadie,' he groaned, taking her hands and raising them to his lips, kissing her fingertips. 'You always were. I've fallen in love with you, too. Can't you see that?'

Sadie froze, spellbound. He loved her? Could it be true?

'I should have told you that before,' he rushed on, 'but I was scared too. I'm a risk for you, because you've been let down before and because I'll always carry a scar in here.'

He pressed a fist to his chest, over his heart.

'It doesn't matter,' she croaked, dizzy with the love she felt for him in return, but he placed his thumb gently over her lips.

'You know that I will always love Karolina and Miko,' he said, sombre. 'That's a lot for any woman to take on. But if you can trust me, I'll show you every day that there's room in here—' he grasped her hand and pressed it to his chest '—to love you and Milly, too. And I love you both, just as much.'

At his wonderful words, Sadie allowed the tears of joy to fall.

Roman cupped her cheeks, swiping them with his thumbs. 'You asked me not to over-promise. But this is a promise I can keep: I love you. You've given me a second chance to be a dad, showed that I deserved a second chance to fall in love, and if you allow me to be a part of your life, yours and Milly's, I promise to show you every day that you can trust me to love you for ever.'

'Roman, I do trust you,' Sadie whispered, her throat thick and hot. 'Let's go home.'

They took a taxi, kissing in the back seat, touching each other in reverent silence.

Milly was at her grandparents' for the night, with Grace, so the minute the door closed, they kissed some more, tugging at each other's clothes as they headed for the bedroom.

'How can I have missed you so much in two days?' he said, kissing a path down her neck, across her chest, sucking first one nipple and then the other.

Sadie tangled her hands in his hair, whispering, 'I love you. I missed you too.'

Roman pressed another fierce kiss to her lips, holding her close. 'Sadie...loving you, loving our daughter, has brought the unscarred parts of my heart back to life.'

He entwined his fingers with hers, his stare searing her soul. 'I want you to wake up every day of our future and believe that, by being at your side, I'm exactly where I want to be. That I choose you. I choose us.'

'I will.' She nodded, reaching for his lips with hers, committing his promises to memory.

In the end, with the right person, believing in dreams was easy.

Pressing her hand to his chest, she rolled him over, straddling his hips so she could pepper his face, his neck, his chest with kisses.

Sadie stared into his beautiful blue eyes, getting lost and finding home. 'When you look at me, when we're alone, just staring, I feel loved for the person I am.'

'You are loved,' he said, drawing her back for another kiss. 'How long have we got?' he asked, curling his fingers through her hair as she pressed a path of kisses down his abdomen.

'Milly will be home at nine, so until then, you're mine.'

Things were just getting hot when he tugged her to a stop.

'Wait.' He drew her into his arms and rolled them, so he was once more on top.

With breath-stealing tenderness, he pressed his lips to hers. 'Happy Valentine's Day.' His voice was low with desire, love shining in his eyes.

Sadie shuddered, everything she felt for this man welling up inside her chest. 'Happy Valentine's Day.'

'I didn't get you a card, or flowers,' he said, pressing kisses of apology along her jaw and down the side of her neck.

Sadie cupped his face, staring deep into his eyes. 'I don't want those things.'

Now that she'd been brave enough to build a future with Roman, all the red roses and heart-shaped cards in the world meant nothing. She had something more important and precious: a family, a man she loved, who loved her in return.

'You are the best Valentine I could ask for,' she said, closing her eyes as he groaned and rained kisses on her face, losing herself in the love they'd found together, love that would always be enough.

EPILOGUE

Fourteen months later

LAUGHING, ROMAN SNAPPED A photo of Milly with his phone. His girl was covered in a fine dusting of icing sugar, squealing excitedly as she brandished a wooden spoon in the air like a flag. Blobs of chocolate icing hit the kitchen bench, the tiled floor and even Milly's blonde head.

'Oh-oh…' Roman said, scooping Milly up and transporting her to the sink where he managed to de-bulk the worst of the cake ingredients from his daughter while she unsuspectingly slashed the wooden spoon through the stream of warm water.

'Tatínek is going to be in trouble with Mummy. Unless we can clean up all of this mess before she gets out of the bath.'

Roman cherished every second with his girls, the ordinary and extraordinary. They enabled him to reflect on how lucky he was to have the love he'd found with his two families, strengthened his vow never to take any moment for granted.

'Clean what up?' Sadie said from the hallway as she entered the decimated kitchen, her smile, as always, brightening his day.

'Just a little baking detritus,' Roman said, placing their toddler on her own two feet so he could wrap his arm around Sadie's waist and kiss her as thoroughly as possible while keeping one eye on Milly.

With a toddler awake and exploring, couple moments were rare. But in the year or so they'd been together, and with the help of Grace and both sets of grandparents, they'd somehow managed to carve out a little grown-up time among all the wonderfully normal everyday family moments.

'What did you bake?' Sadie said a little breathlessly, her eyes scanning the cluttered counter where he'd used every single bowl and utensil they owned.

'A cake!' Roman once more picked up Milly and, with a flourish, whisked off the tea towel covering their creation. 'Ta-da.'

Sadie chuckled, covering her mouth with her hand as she tried to hide her laughter.

'What?' Roman said, admiring the lopsided and partially burned cake. 'So you think it's funny, huh?'

Impatient, he'd put the butter-cream icing on too soon while the cake had still been warm and it was starting to melt, but hopefully it would still taste good.

Slinging his arm around Sadie's shoulder, he drew her close, calculating the hours until Milly's bedtime when he and Sadie could be alone.

'Well, I mean, it's not that funny,' Sadie said, reaching up to kiss Milly's floury cheek. 'It has a certain charm… I mean…if you like burned cake that is, which fortunately I do, so that's good.'

'Oh-oh.' Roman rounded his eyes at Milly. 'Mummy's doing the nervous-chatter thing.'

Because he couldn't be this close to Sadie and not kiss her, he snagged her lips, brushing them with his in a tease, a promise of more to come.

'What are we celebrating?' Sadie asked breathlessly, staring up at him with the passion that was never far away when they were together.

'Nothing in particular,' he said, dipping his finger in the icing and dabbing it first on Milly's nose and then on Sadie's, the sound of their laughter squeezing another drop of love from his heart. 'Just a celebration of us three, and how lucky we are to have each other.'

Sadie sobered, her shining eyes dipping to his mouth just before she gripped his face and kissed him again, this time winding her arms around his neck and pressing her body to his restlessly.

'I love you,' she said, the look she shot him full of heat and promise.

'I love you too,' he said, scooping his arm around her waist, so she couldn't escape, 'which is why I think you should marry me.'

He ignored Sadie's shocked gasp and turned to Milly. 'You think Mummy should marry me too, don't you?'

Milly garbled something unintelligible, waving her wooden spoon in agreement.

'See,' he said, facing Sadie once more. 'She agrees.'

Placing Milly on the floor, he got down on one knee and took Sadie's hand. 'Sadie, it's time to promise we'll be together for ever…you, me and Milly. Will you marry me?'

Laughing through her tears, Sadie kneeled on the floor in front of him, throwing her arms around his shoulders. 'Yes, I will.'

She kissed him, hugged Milly and then kissed him again.

There was flour on the floor, a cupboard spilling out pots and pans. Not the most romantic setting for a proposal, but, for Roman, it was perfect. And he'd make it up to Sadie later, when they were alone.

Roman gripped Sadie's waist and pulled her close, holding both his girls. 'I'd say that was something worth celebrating, wouldn't you?'

Sadie rested her head on his shoulder with a contented sigh. 'Absolutely. Every day with you is worth celebrating.'

* * * * *

If you enjoyed this story, check out these other great reads from
JC Harroway

Phoebe's Baby Bombshell
Breaking the Single Mom's Rules
Tempted by the Rebel Surgeon
How to Resist the Single Dad

All available now!